LEXI GREENE

Bachelor on Board

This book was professionally typeset on Reedsy.
Find out more at reedsy.com

To my brilliant colleague and friend, Fiona Bardenhagen.
May you rest in peace.

Foreword

Success is the best revenge.

Amber Reed, a rising television producer, needs her new show—Bachelor on Board, Australia—to outshine the one her ex stole from her, or risk losing her job to the conniving Lothario, but when her Bachelor falls in love and absconds with one of the contestants, she's forced to rely on Plan B, Nathan Moretti, the high school popular who broke her heart.

Nathan Moretti, soon-to-be head of the wealthy Moretti family, needs a wife to protect the family fortune from his gold-digger stepmother, and his job should be easy with twenty-four beautiful women to choose from. Right?

Not when the only woman he wants is the one behind the camera and her success relies on him finding love with someone else, on screen, on schedule, as promised. Can Amber forgive the past and risk her heart—again?

Acknowledgement

A huge thank you to my fabulous editor Jena O'Connor and my awesome cover designer Charmaine Ross! And to the gorgeous Beverley Eikli and Nina Campbell for their endless support.

Chapter 1

"We've got a problem."

Amber Reed freeze-framed the latest Bachelor of the moment on her computer screen before glancing at her assistant producer, Cassie. "What now? A broken fingernail? The wrong brand of mineral water?"

"Here, I bought you a coffee." Cassie settled a black takeaway cup from Amber's favourite Sydney café in front of her with a shaking hand.

"Thanks, you're a life saver." Amber reached for the cup and sniffed. Ahhh. Vanilla hazelnut cream latte with a shot of caramel. She sipped and closed her eyes to better savour the burst of flavours on her tongue. "Okay, you've got my attention."

No sound. None. Like Cassie had morphed into stone. The silence grabbed Amber by the throat, and her eyes snapped open.

Cassie jumped like she'd been struck. "Dan had this delivered—personally."

She waved a piece of paper in front of Amber, the slight crackle like the first lick of a wildfire before it got greedy.

"What is it?" Amber's gaze dropped to the super-hot bachelor on the screen in front of her. Dan's dimpled smile was guaranteed to break the heart of any woman with a sniff of oestrogen in her body. Charismatic rascal oozed from every pore. The perfect guy for the job. This was it. Her chance to prove to the network executives she had the creative balls to play with the big boys. Jason might have stolen her brightest and shiniest idea—and sold it to them as his own—but success was the sweetest revenge. She was the woman behind *Bachelor on Board, Australia*, and this show would outshine what had been hers, or she would die trying. Nothing could spoil this moment. Nothing. The warmth of the cup in her hands seeped into her soul and the sweet vanilla scent promised all kinds of wonderful, even as the muscles in her neck tightened and the pulse in her temple became a hammer-like throb.

"Here." Cassie shoved the paper towards her like it had grown a tail and a forked tongue and dropped it onto Amber's desk.

The follicles of Amber's skin lifted and something slippery slid along her spine.

Whatever it was, she'd deal with it. It would be fine.

Her grip tightened on the cardboard cup, and she clung to the lingering sense of oh-so-good. Her gaze dropped to the first sentence. "He's left?" she spluttered. "He can't leave. We have a contract." The letters leapt about like black sin on virginal white. The cup crushed in her hand and hot liquid splashed onto her skin. "Ouch."

She lowered it to her desk, and Cassie thrust tissues towards her to mop up the mess.

"This wasn't part of the deal. He gets married on screen at the end of the series, as promised." How could a renowned bachelor fall in love at first sight—before the uber-expensive superyacht they'd chartered for the show had even left the dock—and leave her in the lurch? "No. This can't be happening. Besides, Christina has a contract. Where are they? I need to speak with them."

"Gone. Did you read all the way to the end?"

"No, I didn't get to the end. I'm still choking on the beginning. Not to mention scalding myself."

"Keep reading."

The last few lines were a rocky ravine, a treacherous mountain pass, a canyon to be scaled, and her heart pounded. *My best mate, Nathan, has agreed to take my place. He's an uber-wealthy workaholic who needs more balance in his life. Amber, you're brilliant. If you can find love for me, you can find it for him, too. I thank you from the bottom of my heart.*

"Has the man not heard of 'legally binding'? He can't just pack up and walk out, and leave me with some unknown replacement to fill in. We can't interview and select more women now. We selected them *for him*. Based on *his* astrology. And he's taken off with one of our girls. *Ours!* Not his. Not yet. Not unless it's on national television." She took a giant breath, closed her eyes and all but screamed at herself. *You can do this. It will be okay.*

"This show cannot fail." The words stuck in her throat and she washed them down with a swig of her coffee. "I will not give Jason the satisfaction." The thought of her ex curled her toes and not in a good way—in a tight, cramping, painful way. "Let's get Legal onto this. There has to be a way to get Dan back."

Cassie waved another sheet of paper towards her. "All might not be lost... or it might. What do you think?" She placed a photo on top of the page.

Amber's eyes nearly popped out of her head and ran after

her missing lead man.

No.

Her chest constricted, and she reached for what was left of her coffee. Cassie's voice came to her ears—elongated and distorted like an image from a carnival hall of mirrors.

Nathan *Moretti?*

It was him.

Her cheeks burned and she fanned the flames, gasping for air like a woman who'd come face to face with a ghost from the past. *The man who'd ruined her reputation and left her the laughingstock of her swish Sydney Grammar school.*

Amber took a swig of her coffee and choked as the liquid did its best to drown her. Putting the cup down, she hacked the fluid from her lungs and fought for air. Hellfire and brimstone. She couldn't do this. She couldn't become that hybrid person again, part mouse, part shrinking violet, part shattered glass. She wouldn't.

"I am not letting that wolf loose amongst our girls. There's not a chance. No way. Not going to happen."

"You're right." Cassie's tone was conciliatory, and she reached for the photo. "We'll find some other drop-dead-gorgeous billionaire bachelor willing to pick up where Dan left off by… this afternoon!" She paused for a long moment before adding, "Are you okay? You look green. Pasty. Sweaty."

Amber felt like a bony hand had taken her by the throat and crushed her windpipe. It stole her breath. Give it back, she screamed inside her head. She could do this. She had to. She didn't have a choice. The pressure around her throat eased a smidge and oxygen rushed through. She could do this. She could face Neanderthal Nathan.

"Amber, he's a fire sign. Not Aries like Dan, but Leo. Same.

Same. I'll go through the profiles of the women again. Work out which ones would suit him best." Cassie's voice had a soothing Zen to it. "Dan's given us a list of what Nathan's looking for in a woman."

"An X chromosome." Her tone was sorely bruised. "Which should make our job easy."

The women settled on the motor yacht were women she'd interviewed personally, and she'd promised them a special guy, someone worthy of their yearning hearts, someone who wanted to find the woman of his dreams, someone who wanted marriage and kids and the picket fence. Cassie might be a bit of a hippy with her pink hair and penchant for flared jeans with rhinestones, but she had a way with match-making—she'd worked her charm for Dan. Maybe she could do it again with Nathan.

But to see their carefully selected women laid out like sacrificial offerings at the altar of Neanderthal Nathan? They deserved better. Hell, she'd deserved better. What kind of guy befriended a girl, earned her trust—her love—then slept with her to win *a bet*? And, told all of his jock mates she was a virgin, as if *that* was the crime of the century. Virginity was overrated, like the sexual act. Part A goes into Part B equals a broken heart and a girl shamed. She couldn't even look at his photo without wanting to scratch his eyes from his too-handsome, too-satisfied, too-mocking face.

"There must be another way. Come on. You're a creative. Think of something."

"There isn't." Cassie backed towards the door. "Besides, didn't you say that a man with a dog was the only kind worth loving?"

"What's that got to do with it?" A moment later, an overenthusiastic, short-haired, long-legged mutt whipped through the open doorway and beat a path to her desk in less time than it took her to jump to her feet, open-mouthed.

"Niko, come back here, Niko!" A male voice, deep and booming. A voice that lifted the hair follicles all over her body and chilled her skin, snap-freezing her brain.

The mutt jumped up, his claws catching in the expensive silk weave of her favourite top and because she was stunned, disoriented, still trying to pull time particles together... his wet, sloppy tongue landed on her face. Warm doggy breath thawed her paralysed muscles, and her nose scrunched as she batted him away and swiped at her skin. "What the hell." Her voice came from somewhere deep and dark inside her chest. She struggled to stand and her heels—her beloved Jimmy Choo heels, which she'd taken to wearing since she found herself surrounded by women as tall and lofty as super models—slipped out from beneath her. She fell back, her hip banging against the desk on the way down.

The owner of the booming voice burst into her line of vision and came to an abrupt stop. His dog lavished her carefully made-up face with his wet tongue, and she battled to fend the mutt off and salvage her dignity.

"Oh, I'm sorry." His grin belied his words.

The heavy weight of the beast lifted from her chest, and Amber took a deep, ragged breath into rattling lungs. She'd died and gone to hell.

"Niko, where are your manners?"

The voice resonated through her like a slow, molten wave and the frostiness inside of her was in grave danger of collapse. The dog looked repentant, like he knew he'd done something wrong, but he couldn't hold back his puppy-like exuberance, or that tongue-dripping doggy-smile that wiped every remonstrance from her mind.

"He gets excited when he sees a beautiful woman."

That had to be a well-perfected line. And worse, she felt a laugh bubble in her throat. Where was her damn anger when she needed it?

"He's still a rambunctious puppy. He hasn't had time to grow into his limbs. Niko, get down." The man pulled him further out of reach and held him close.

Amber eyed the diamond-studded collar. Were those real diamonds on that thing? She got to her feet and smoothed her top back into place. She had no choice, but to turn her gaze to the man before her—Neanderthal Nathan. Her breath stilled. Her stomach clenched. Her heart missed a thousand beats and shattered in her chest.

This wasn't happening. This couldn't be happening. Not again. Not when she'd promised herself, she'd never have to see him again. Breathe. The air caught like a shard of glass in her throat. She collapsed into her seat like her bones had turned to dust. No way would she let him know how much he disturbed her. Still.

"Amber? Amber Reed? Is that you?"

Damn. "Nathan Moretti." Her tone oozed prim resistance.

He held the wriggling behemoth of a dog, his blue, blue eyes searching hers from a well-tanned, gorgeous face.

Why had she thought he would ever be interested in her? Because when she was near him, her brain went to mush. She couldn't think. She couldn't coordinate her limbs. She couldn't breathe. Light-headed, she straightened in her seat. It was ten years ago. Ten years. Three thousand, six hundred and fifty days. Eighty-seven thousand, six hundred hours. Not long enough to put the agony of Neanderthal Nathan behind her, it seemed. "What a surprise."

He lowered himself into the chair opposite her, stroking the dog's smooth head. His legs were long and muscular beneath soft designer denim. He propped one leg casually across the other. High-end leather loafers. His black shirt fitted him snugly, showing off a torso that was wide at the shoulders, narrow at the waist, and his open collar boasted a tanned, muscular... oh, stop. This wasn't healthy. She reached for her coffee and breathed the aroma as she might nitrous oxide.

"You haven't changed." Her smile-that-wasn't-a-smile took an inordinate amount of effort. She eyed him like she might an eight-legged interloper, or a man who had one hell of a cheek strolling into her office like he belonged there.

"You're barely recognisable. What happened to the Morticia Addams look?"

"Nathan, can I get you a coffee?" Cassie's voice came to her ears from a distance, like the sizeable room had narrowed to a single point filled with man and memories.

"No thanks, I'm good." He winked and shot Cassie a dimpled grin.

Amber watched her feisty assistant wilt under the force of it. Charm, pure and lethal, honed with deadly precision. Women were pathetic when it came to Nathan. And then it struck her. Nathan owed her. He owed her big time. Maybe all wasn't lost.

"You do understand that you have to date twenty-four women on national television and find one you're willing to marry, preferably on screen? No eloping," she added through gritted teeth.

"I do."

The pun was accompanied by dimples, double-barrelled and aimed her way. "Why would you do that? What's in it for you? Aren't you a confirmed bachelor, party-boy, happy-go-lucky… " *shmuck?*

"Besides a beautiful woman or twenty-four?" His face beamed, and his smile? His smile could take out a battalion of women at two hundred feet. White, white teeth. Killer dimples. Eyes so blue, so crystal clear, so smoking hot, she had to fight the blast of memories and the visceral punch to her gut.

She waved her latte under her nose and breathed the sweet scent of it, grounding herself firmly on her side of the desk. "Last I checked, you weren't short of a woman or two or twenty-four." Her own smile tasted saccharine. His sexual exploits were well known to anyone who paid attention to the social pages. He was one of the most eligible bachelors in Sydney—*the* most eligible bachelor in Sydney. Her pulse picked up. Her mind raced. "There are less public ways of finding a wife."

Cassie mimed pleading motions behind him.

"Maybe I'm looking for fame."

Cassie fanned her face like she had a raging temperature, or her hormones were on fire, or her ovaries had exploded.

Amber ignored Cassie's theatrics and pinned her gaze on the oh-so-casually slouched man in front of her. "I think we both know you have that in spades. What's truly riding on this?" Her heartbeat hammered in her ears, the sound deafening as his smile faltered. How could she allude to *The Bet*? What was she thinking? She needed him. She hated to think it let alone say it, but she was desperate, and he was the most eligible bachelor in Sydney. A coup for the show. She needed him. She needed this show to be a success. Her credibility was on the line.

"Product placement. I want the girls to drink my protein shakes and super green smoothies, take my vitamins, and use my skin care range."

Typical. It wasn't like he needed the advertising.

It was hot in here. Too hot. She lifted her long hair off her neck and dragged it to one side. "So, it's all about business for you and how many more billions we can help you make?"

"Look, do you need me to step in for Dan or not?" He rose to his feet, and she found herself leaping to her own.

"I do, but I have the pristine hearts of twenty-four beautiful women to protect. You're to treat them with respect and leave the adolescent behaviour on dry land. If you genuinely want to find a partner, if you genuinely want to fall in love, if you genuinely want to get married... I want you on the show. If not? I want you as far away as possible. Are we clear?"

"Crystal." His gaze stripped her of everything. Clothes, dignity, and false bravado. "I've got my gear in the car, and I can find my way to Circular Quay. I'll see you on board." He saluted her with a boyish grin. "I always wanted to be a movie star."

Her body lit up like a Christmas tree. Holy smoke. Blue blazes. Breathe.

"This isn't exactly Hollywood."

"You don't mind if Niko joins us, do you? I reckon he'll help me sort the good from the bad pretty quickly. He sure likes you."

Amber almost choked on her tongue, before it dashed out to wet her lips. Damn it. She needed to get it together.

"We weren't anticipating a canine guest. Does he get sea-sick?" She smoothed her top over the well-fitted waist of her pencil skirt. "We don't have time to recruit new bachelorettes.

The girls we chose for Dan will have to do for you. We'll get the girls we sent home after the first two episodes to come back. I'll go over what's required of you in a couple of hours. There's a lot to be done and you need to meet your host, Cory."

"Don't worry. Dan gave me the lowdown. I'm raring to go. Meet and greet. Cocktail party. Key ceremony." He ticked them off on his fingers. His hand was large, masculine, tanned and strong, yet capable of incredible finesse, if her memory served her correctly. A fresh wave of heat flowed through her, and she lifted her hair from her neck.

"And he's boat-trained. He uses puppy pads. They work a treat."

"Of course, he does. Good. Then we need to get you to wardrobe. Make-up. Rehearsal. There's no time to waste. We have to reshoot the first couple of episodes, so our timeframe, which was already impossibly tight, just got tighter. You're in for some late nights."

"Bring it on." He let go of Niko, and the dog bolted from the room. There was no bolting from her smug, soon-to-be star, who swaggered towards the door, with a smile over his shoulder. So, he knew the effect he had on her and if she wasn't mistaken, she'd just gifted her soul to the very devil who stole her heart.

Nate struggled to settle the wriggling, writhing bundle of dog onto the soft leather seat of his late model Italian sports car. He strapped the seat belt across Niko's body, muttering a demand to stay still. Amber Reed. Who'd have thought? Dan had mentioned a beautiful, green-eyed, blonde-haired producer, but Nate hadn't been prepared for the blast of memories that left him gaping and hollow. He'd had a plan. Go on some dates and get some product exposure for his younger sister's business, and the clinic that saved her life. Woo a woman who'd make a compatible wife, willing to sign a prenuptial agreement—and gain control of the family business as per his grandfather's will. He wasn't a fool, and he wasn't his father. No way would *he* fall for a gold-digger, nor let the woman spend her way through their hard-earned fortune. Amber Reed was a major hitch. Or not. He owed her, and now he could repay all of his debts with one sleight of hand *and* find a wife. Smooth.

So why the sense of impending disaster? Her black phase might be over, and she may have transformed into a willowy blonde bombshell, but he'd crossed her once before, and he wasn't in a hurry to repeat the experience. He'd probably deserved every ill-fated thing that had happened since. It wasn't like she was responsible for the shark that attacked them. Dan had physical scars, his flesh torn saving Nate's life, but Nate was scarred, too. On the inside. He'd struggled to get back into the water—he'd started with pictures of sharks, then progressed to watching them at the aquarium, and finally to standing in the domed glass area where the sharks swam over him and around him, but not with him. He'd been determined to overcome his fear. Determined to get back into the surf. And he had.

He was alive because of Dan and what Dan had suffered for him. He should be grateful to Amber. He owed her twofold. She'd introduced his mate to Christina, and Dan had never been happier. And twenty-four women were good odds. Grateful, that's what he should be.

Shaking the morbid thoughts from his mind, he manoeuvred himself into the busy afternoon traffic along Elizabeth Street.

The car raced like a thoroughbred beneath his touch, raring to go, revving loudly with the slightest coaxing from his foot on the accelerator. The sky was clear, the sun beat down on the shiny black enamel of his vehicle, and he was looking forward to a bit of fun. Beautiful women. Fine food. Being the first *Bachelor on Board* had a ring to it. He could live with that.

Besides, his sister's cause could do with the burst of publicity. It was one thing to run his grandfather's successful empire and provide for his family, it was another thing entirely to help his sister build a business and mentor troubled teens. The business did more than provide them with a job—it gave them a sense of autonomy and purpose and belonging. It did way more for their self-esteem than a donation could. This way, they experienced the thrill of building a business from the ground up. Their success was their own, even if he had a hand in steering it. How did the saying go? *Give a man a fish, and you feed him for a day. Teach a man to fish, and you feed him for a lifetime.*

He pulled into busy Circular Quay and whistled when he saw the seventy-five metre Benetti superyacht. She was sleek and glamorous, and towered above the smaller ferries and tour boats. The Harbour Bridge arched across the sky to his left, and over to his right, the Opera House gleamed white.

Nate clipped Niko's lead to his collar and reached into the back for his suitcase. He took a deep breath of the warm afternoon air, tangy with salt from the sea, and adjusted his sunglasses on his face. The path stretched ahead, bordered by grass and blasts of purple from the Jacaranda trees in full bloom. Spring was a great time of year. A fellow stood watching him, his gaze expectant. Of course, Amber would have phoned ahead.

"Hello, you must be Nathan. I'm Cory. Nice wheels." The man's gaze lingered on the sleek, sexy vehicle. "Are you planning on leaving it there?" He nodded towards the no-standing sign.

"Nope. I've got my second in charge coming to pick her up." Nate stepped forward to shake Cory's hand. "Nice to meet you. I hear we get to share this not-too-shabby vessel with a posse of beautiful women."

"Indeed, we do."

Niko leapt onto the man's schmick suit pants, and Nate struggled to hold him back, soothing the fretful, excitable animal. "Sorry, he's still a bit young and crazy."

"No worries. Let's get you on board. Amber plans to give you an hour or so to settle in before she arrives, clipboard in hand, ready to spin her magic and create amazing TV."

"She knows her job then?"

"You're in very good hands. Oh, and I've arranged for one of the crew to take Niko for a run. Here he is now."

"Thank you. I wasn't sure how Niko would manage on the boat, but he's toilet trained, and he's an important part of my strategy." Nate handed the straining dog over to a young man in white shorts and a white top. He took the lead with a grin, and Niko wagged his tail so hard his whole body got in on the act. "I'll see you soon, buddy." Nate stroked Niko's head, his coat like smooth velvet beneath his touch, then walked with Cory towards the ramp leading up to the deck. "Where are the girls?"

"They're settled into their rooms on the main deck. We're on the upper deck. Thanks for stepping up, bro. We'd be in a mountain of a mess without you."

"Yeah, well, twenty-four beauties and cruising. How hard

can it be?"

Cory grinned as he ushered Nate into the grand foyer. "Man, you've got the toughest job on the planet. That's a lot of women to sift through. You'll send four ladies home tonight after the cocktail party. How's your small talk?"

"I've had twenty-eight years to perfect it." Nate grinned.

"I hope you find love, because Amber deserves a break, and if you take off like Dan did?" Cory's eyes held his for long enough to burn. "I'll hunt you down."

"I want to find a woman to marry, and I owe Amber. I'm not going anywhere." The show was important to her? Of course, it was.

"This is a tough industry. You don't get too many chances. And this beauty…" he gestured around the luxurious lounge with the shiny Italian marble floors, polished timber finishes, and gold fittings "…doesn't come cheap."

Nate nodded and a tiny seed of apprehension took root.

"Do you socialise with the women yourself?" Cory was a good-looking guy who clearly worked out. "Is there a gym on board?"

"No, they're all yours, and yes…" Cory grinned. "The gym is down on the lower deck in the beach club, along with a lounge and bar, yoga studio, steam room, and sauna. And there's a couple of pools and jacuzzis on board. You and Dan look about the same size. That should make wardrobe happy. It's two o'clock now. We'll need to get you into makeup by three and dressed by four-thirty. There won't be any briefing about the women except for photos and names."

"Twenty-four, huh?"

"Yep. How's your memory?"

"When it comes to beautiful women, exceptional." Nate's

stomach churned. Since the moment he'd entered Amber's office, there was only one beautiful woman on his mind, and she wasn't the quiet type. Words from the past echoed in his ears. Deeds from the past twisted in his gut, sharp with regret. But worse by far, was his body's reaction.

"Good. Follow me, and I'll show you around. You're upstairs in the stateroom and master suite."

This beauty was to be his home for the next six weeks. He couldn't complain.

"Who would have thought Dan would find 'the one' and walk away?" Cory commented as he stepped ahead.

Nate wasn't surprised by that at all. Dan had changed after the attack. They both had. Dan took nothing for granted. If he'd found the woman of his dreams, he wouldn't go through the farce of dating anyone else, nor waste a moment of his precious time. He was a genuine, decent man who deserved to be happy, and Nate was glad for him, but he didn't plan on falling in love. Not even for Amber Reed.

Ratings success? That, he owed her.

His heart? Not a snowball's chance in hell.

Amber stood on the aft main deck and shaded her eyes from the sun. The sail-like roof of the Opera House gleamed, and on the waterfront, people bustled about or sat at tables with wine and food. Her hands shook, and her tummy fluttered, but she straightened her spine and lifted her chin.

You can do this. You're okay. You've got this.

Ambers heels snapped against the glossy Italian marble floor as she made her way into the enormous, carpeted lounge area where the girls sat on plush leather couches, dressed and ready. Amber let the sound of the music from the baby grand piano wash over her and her gaze scanned the opulent space. The walls were covered with dark wallpaper gilded with gold, above polished wood panelling. There was a beautiful marble fireplace with gas-generated flame, a massive, gilded mirror, and enormous floor to ceiling windows. French doors led out to an open terrace and an amazing view of Sydney Harbour. With the doors open, a warm sea-kissed breeze permeated the luxurious space. Everything looked picture perfect except for the shallow frowns at the edges of the smooth brows before her.

Amber gave Catherine a reassuring smile. According to Cassie, she was an Aries and would make a terrific partner for Nate. Both fire signs. Both passionate and energetic.

"I have news." Amber waited until she had everyone's attention. "Unfortunately, Dan has left the show." There was a communal gasp of surprise and a burst of animated chatter. Amber waited for the wave of reaction to settle. "But we do have a new bachelor and tonight's cocktail party will go ahead as planned, after we reshoot the meet and greet."

"So that's why you asked us to dress in the same clothes and hair styles," Catherine said, and Amber turned towards her.

"Yes. Consider the first one a rehearsal. The women Dan sent home have returned and they'll re-join you shortly, but four women will leave the ship tonight. The choice of who goes home is up to Nathan. That means a late night. I'll need you on the dock in five minutes. We won't need to reshoot the scenes in the limo. We'll reshoot the footage from the top of the path. Your new bachelor's name is Nathan Moretti."

"Not *the* Nathan Moretti?" Twenty-four gasps merged into one. "The hunky squillionaire?" Catherine's voice.

"The man himself." Amber ignored the sharp arrow-twist of

pain in her chest and the stir of reaction in the pit of her belly. She had no interest in Nathan and every interest in making this show a success. She would find him the perfect woman, he would propose to her on screen, and the ratings would soar.

She heard his name being whispered amongst the women with a hint of adoration. "He's gorgeous. Oh my God. This is the opportunity of a lifetime."

If she could pull this off, her career would be made.

When she pulled this off, her career would be made, and she could return to her small hometown, Lilydale, with her head held high. Six short weeks. She could do that. She could put up with Neanderthal Nathan for six short weeks.

Chapter Two

The high heeled, glamorous group of women walked en masse along the dock towards the busy, tree-lined street where Amber could see Cassie waiting with a clipboard. Behind her was a huddle of film studio trucks, and a shanty town of fold-up chairs and tables. The women's excited chatter carried on the warm evening air, along with the honey-sweet scent of the flowering Jacaranda trees that lined the quay.

The glow of the sun clung to the horizon by the merest thread, the rich cobalt blue of twilight spreading like ink across the sky. The buildings behind the women rose like sparkling stalagmites, and across the dark splotch of the sea to her left, people bustled on their way to the ferries and bars and restaurants. A boat horn sounded, hollow and coarse, and a Paramatta-Darling Harbour ferry inched out of its berth at Wharf five, it's engine revving, the propellers stirring the water, sending waves to splash against the sea wall.

Amber wanted the lighting to be perfect and she had maybe five minutes to get Nathan into position. The camera crew was just about ready, and John gave her a thumbs-up. She checked in with Cassie, who assured her the ladies were in position and ready to go. Jacquie would meet Nathan first.

Cory and Nathan were moments away. Phew. She took a deep calming breath. *You've got this.* She closed her eyes and breathed the spicy fragrances from the nearby restaurants. The hum of traffic was loud in the background and there was the promise of a cool night. It had been a hot day for spring and the weather was perfect for filming. Warm enough to be outside, but not so roasting that the girls' makeup would slip and slide. Not a breath of wind. The girls' hair arrangements were safe. All would be fine. She could do this. Nathan had given his word he would see this through. Not that his word was particularly reliable. Amber shook the thought away. She fully planned to keep him in her sight at all times. She couldn't afford to have another bachelor go missing in action. She'd moved onto the massive motor yacht and would keep a close eye on her leading man until they sailed. Besides, filming would go late into the night. This show would be a success—or she would die trying. Success was about grit, not luck.

Amber shook herself into action and briefed the camera crew. The atmosphere around her buzzed. She loved the air of creative possibility. The promise of magic. She just had to ensure the cameras caught every nuance, every quiet moment. Her senses were on hyper alert. Her mind was sharp and focused, which was why she knew the moment Nathan stepped onto the dock. It had nothing to do with the past and everything to do with finding the perfect woman to thaw his cold heart. And capture it on film. This could be it. Her moment to shine. She would make it happen. She wanted it more than she'd wanted anything in her life. Even Nathan. Back then.

Back then, she'd been naïve and foolish. Reckless. Now she was sophisticated and layered and wise. She spun on her heels and nearly fell off them when her gaze clashed with his. Her knees buckled. Blue blazes. Nathan in denim was dangerous. Nathan in a tuxedo was lethal.

"Hello again." Nathan's voice was deep and gravelly and sexy, and too confident for her liking, but he was her lead man and confidence was good.

"Hello." She forced steel into her bones and stood tall, her gaze ensnared in the blue trap of his. "You washed up just fine."

"Where do you want me?" He grinned—cocky—like he knew what churned inside of her. "Cory tells me the lighting is right and we need to move."

"Yes. Yes, it is." She couldn't find her words. She couldn't think. Her cheeks heated, and her skin beaded with sweat like she'd stepped too close to open flame. She might be a blonde—now—but she still had her red-head propensity to blush. Her heart pounded, and she clung onto her clipboard like it was the land that pitched and rolled instead of the sea. Hell, she was twenty-six years old, not a naïve sixteen-year-old swept off her feet by a final-year Lothario. She was all grown up. An adult. Breathe. She was in charge. And she wouldn't let him steal her mojo. She needed it. Now.

"Positions. Let's get moving and Nathan…" She gave him a small device to situate in his ear. "We'll be in contact at all times. The first contestant is Jacquie. She's about a moment away. You just need to introduce yourself and she'll do the same, then she'll walk up the gangway and wait for you inside."

"I know the drill." His eyes said he knew exactly what curled inside of her like a traitorous cat to his hungry dog. "I'm ready when you are."

Amber gritted her teeth and held on to her clipboard with white knuckles. She watched as the meet-and-greet unfolded without a hitch, woman by woman, and the knots in her spine began to loosen. He was a natural. Relaxed. Charming. Smoking hot. The women couldn't hide their admiration or their interest. Sexual attraction sparked like fireworks in the night sky. Not one contestant failed to show pleasant surprise and like Cassie, each visibly softened and glowed with a delightful mix of awkward attraction except for maybe two or three of the more extroverted girls who came out with guns blazing, flirting up a storm.

She didn't need the reminder of what it felt like to watch Nathan with another woman. He'd moved straight on to Bethany, one of the most popular senior girls, after his humiliating *win*, and she'd slunk around the school, trying to ignore the mocking smirks from all and sundry.

It was excruciating to watch but watch she would.

Not only watch, she would encourage and stoke and do everything in her power to ensure one of these women won his heart.

Whoa. These women were amazing. Stunning. And some were super-intelligent as well as super-gorgeous. He could see it in the depths of their perfectly made-up faces. Others were fun and frisky, with the confidence that came from knowing they were attractive and desirable. Then there were the introverted ones who struggled to look him in the eyes, but who stoked his interest anyway. He'd lost count, but they kept coming. In black. In red. In virginal white, their curves a delicious temptation. He fought to maintain his focus.

Every woman deserved their moment to feel special, to feel seen. He wanted each and every one of them to know he'd paid attention. It seemed only fair when they'd put themselves

22

out there on national television. He knew how important it was to remember their names. He'd studied their names and photos for long enough to have a pretty good grasp of them, but in the flesh? Two dimensional photos didn't capture the full impact of a woman.

"Three to go." Amber's voice washed over him like a warm wave, and memories swamped him. The feel of her skin—soft and smooth—and the sensual sound of her breath. The way his body had reacted like he'd never truly touched a girl before, or since.

"This is Suzanne."

He liked Amber's voice in his ear. He liked it a lot. A woman sauntered towards him like a black-eyed panther, her gaze on his, and his breath stilled in his chest.

"Hi Nate." Invitation was rife in her violet eyes. She leaned in to kiss him on the cheek. Her teeth flashed white as she reached up to wipe the lipstick from his face, her touch lingering.

"Suzanne, nice to meet you. Are you looking forward to some fun?"

"I can't wait." Her gaze smouldered. "I'm looking forward to some one-on-one time later on." He got the sense she would devour him if she got her claws into him and, for the first time, he got a healthy dose of trepidation. Dan had fallen fast and furious. What was to stop him from getting caught up in the crazy as well? And there she was. Amber. His anchor in the storm.

"Nathan, keep her moving. We've got two women to go."

"Well, you head on up and find yourself a drink. I look forward to speaking with you again… soon." He coaxed Suzanne towards the vessel, his hand on her lower back.

"Oh, yes, please." She smiled over her shoulder, her eyelashes dipping. "Nice to meet you, Nathan." She spun back to give him a hug, her words a quiet whisper in his ear. "I wonder if you taste as good as you look."

"I heard that," Amber snapped. "Put her down."

Nate untangled himself from the vine-like woman and delivered her to the gangway.

"Until later." Hell, she'd eat him alive given half the chance, and he just might like it. Schooling his features into a relaxed, charming smile he waited for the next contestant.

A short blonde pixie cut this time. Friendly smile. Tanned and tall.

Nate greeted her with a friendly warmth he hadn't felt for the previous contestant. This one was delightfully clumsy, and she tripped at the last moment, falling straight into his arms. Artfully in hindsight, yet spontaneous and genuine.

"I'm so sorry," she gushed. "I'm Nina. Nice to meet you. Damn heels. I'm not used to them. I'm a zoologist, you see. I'm more used to boots. Too much information. Right? Sorry. Hi." She stepped away from him, but he kept hold of her hand. Her skin was silky and soft, and her nails, trimmed short, were polished with a high-gloss finish.

"Nice to meet you, Nina." He lifted her hand for a kiss, and her delicious chocolate brown gaze clung to his. She was cute and flustered. "I don't know how any woman manages to walk in those things."

"They're a killer," she said with a laugh. "I'm glad I'm not a model."

"You could be." He gave her an appreciative once-over, his gaze slipping from her decadent eyes, along her glossy red dress (was that thing vinyl?) to her killer red heels.

"Oh, thank you." Her cheeks flushed pink. "It's nice to meet you, too. I don't suppose you could help me up that ramp."

He laughed aloud as he ushered her up the gangway. "Perhaps you'd better find a seat in there until I can come to your rescue."

"Oh, that's a good plan. I'm a walking disaster."

He chuckled to himself as he strode back to his position. He liked a woman who could laugh at herself and not take this circus too seriously. The lights blinded him completely, and he was oblivious to the cameras and the crew in the darkness beyond.

"That was great," Amber said with an encouraging laugh. "Keep it up. One more to go, and we'll take you inside. The mozzies are a killer out here, but don't worry, you're safe with me around. My blood is delectable."

Delectable was exactly how he remembered her, but their friendship and foolish foray into sexual territory was tainted by the awfulness that had followed. To this day, he was ashamed of his behaviour. Teenage boys didn't think with their head—a fact all mothers should share with their teenage daughters. He was relieved to hear the click of heels on the concrete path and to be distracted from the direction of his thoughts. Now was not the time.

"Hello." A tinkling voice this time, and he found himself at the mercy of yet another buxom beauty. It was like every man's fantasy. Attractive women, lots of them, all focused on him. His own personal harem. The teenage boy within would have been in his element, but Nate was all grown up, and he'd learned that women hurt deeply. Everything had changed post-Amber. Life had grabbed him by the balls and taught him a lesson or five or six, and they were lessons he'd needed to learn. But that didn't make them any less brutal.

Breathe.

Amber forced air into her constricted lungs. "Cut. Terrific. Well done, Nathan. Let's go on board now." He gave her the kind of smile that left a woman wanting foolish things. Like a closer connection. There was a gravity in his gaze, a humility she scarcely recognised it was so unexpected. When he spoke to her, his gaze didn't just capture hers, it promised his full attention. Neanderthal Nathan appeared… civilised. It was there in his manners. In the respect he'd shown for each of the women. He'd been polite, yes, but it was more than that. He'd seemed aware of their vulnerability. Of his position of power. Amber felt like a feather in a cyclonic wind. Dizzy. Torn. Buffeted, until she didn't know which way was up.

But she knew better than to believe what was sugar-coated and wrapped to please. Hopefully, he really had changed, but she didn't trust the wolf in him. He didn't just desire a woman, he hungered for her. He didn't just take a woman, he ravaged her. He made a woman feel… irresistible. Coveted.

Amber shook the whimsical nonsense from her thoughts and consulted with the camera crew to ensure they had full coverage of the vessel. She wanted every intimate and catty moment on film. When she entered the lounge, the girls seemed to have multiplied. They sat on the soft leather couches or stood chatting. Some had moved out through the French doors and onto the generous deck, but each held an obligatory glass of champagne in hand. A few of them would be on to their second. Or third.

She clapped her hands to capture their attention, her nose crinkling against the barrage of perfumes and hair sprays. "Nathan needs time to get to know each of you and to work out who he wants to send home tonight. Equally important, *you* need to consider whether Nathan is the man for you. We'll give you as much space as we can. Nathan has a lot of women to get through so please be respectful of each other."

At least three of the women appeared well-greased for a catfight, their voices raised and sharp. So many women in such a small space, vying for the attention of one very eligible bachelor was sure to end in fireworks. Toughen up, she lectured herself. That was what made for interesting television. The hard truth was that only one woman could win, and twenty-three would have their hopes dashed.

Her compassion would be her undoing. She remembered only too well how hurtful that cut could be, and these women had to endure it on national television. Still, it was a price they were willing to pay. For what? The chance to become a celebrity? To win the heart of a billionaire? High stakes, she supposed. Courage came in many guises. Sometimes as simply as breathing when every cell in your body wanted to die.

Amber was in Nathan's ear, and he was in hers. His sexy baritone stirred her somewhere deep inside and sent shivers over her skin. She didn't like it. She didn't like the way her body reacted to the gravelly tone of his voice. She didn't like the way she was intrigued by his warm friendliness. Who was this man? Where was the over-indulged, high-on-daddy's-money teenager she'd enjoyed sparring with? Until she hadn't—he'd devoured her innocence and spat out her bones. But this man paid attention. He listened. He appeared genuinely interested in each of the girls. He took the time to help them relax, to ask them how they were feeling. This man was generous and genuine in his praise of an outfit or a hair style. Was it just for the camera? She couldn't know, but she did know he was the perfect bachelor for the show. Excitement battled with nerves as he presented the stateroom's gold key to one of her favourite girls, Mia. The key came with a gold heart attached.

She could do this. If he kept doing what he was doing, the show would be a success. She could practically reach out and feel it. She could make this show something special.

"Nathan, it's time to say good-bye. We need to get to the elimination ceremony."

"One more. I can't leave anyone out. Catherine looks downhearted, and I can't have that. Besides, I want the chance to get to know her better."

"Right." Amber was lost for words. "Five minutes. Tops."

Nathan walked over to Catherine, who visibly melted with relief, and despite herself Amber warmed a degree. So, he'd developed a conscience. The man was twenty-eight years old. He had to have evolved over time. Besides, he was coming from a very low base.

Teenagers were hormones with feet. Information she could have used back then. She'd fallen for his smarmy lines, his false smile, his magnetism, and she'd held nothing back. She'd trusted him. She'd lost herself in him. She'd given him everything, and he'd given her... fool's gold in exchange for the most precious thing a girl could give. Not her virginity, which was a physiological thing and who cared anyway, but the openness of her heart and the purity of her love. Never again would she love without holding a piece of herself back. Scars. They ran deep and for twenty-three of these women, she feared the longer they stayed, the harder they'd fall.

She listened as Nathan wielded pleasantries with a charm and charisma that ignited a glow in every woman within his vicinity. He was exceptional, and she intuited his moves were highly practiced. He appeared casual and relaxed. He soothed with the touch of his hand or the way he angled his body to focus on one woman and her alone. Each and every woman's nervous mannerisms eased. Visibly. He was a magician and for every woman, he conjured the illusion that she stood out from the rest. Special and desirable. Oh, he was good.

"Cut."

Nathan ignored Amber's call and whispered something into Catherine's ear.

"I said cut." Age-old resentment uncoiled inside her and flashed its fangs. Maybe those wounds weren't as healed as she'd hoped. No, he couldn't hurt her. Not now. Not ever again. She was in charge. She was the boss. This was *her* show.

"Nathan, you need to move out into the foyer area. Consider each of the girls' photos and work out which four you'd like to send home. I'll get the girls organised for the key ceremony."

"Already decided, Boss. Let's get on with it."

Truly? He'd looked enamoured with all of them. "Right then. Great."

"Girls." Amber spoke aloud to the whole group. Could you all stand over here, please? Leave your glasses." Some of the women wobbled on their heels, and she wondered how much they'd had to drink. With the boat moored at Circular Quay, they could hardly blame the swell. They huddled together in a prickly, well-groomed gaggle, and she couldn't help but feel for the four who would be left exposed at the end. At least they'd have each other. It would be interesting to see who he chose to stay. Would he go for the outrageously flirty types or the deeper, calmer varieties? Each woman was attractive in her own way, but would he appreciate that or go for the stereotypical beauties? "Right. Ready to roll."

Cory addressed the group. He was polished and well-spoken,

and genuinely sobered by the occasion. Four women's hopes would be dashed. Four women would disembark and go home.

Nathan selected the classic and curvaceous beauties first, and Amber stifled a sigh of disappointment. He hadn't changed. Not a smidge. He had the group down to six and they consoled each other with frightened glances. Separated from the pack, they looked vulnerable in their heels, their smiles nervous, their gazes intense as they tried to commune with the man in control of their fate.

"Catherine." He gave the woman a charming smile, and Amber heard her sigh of relief.

She accepted the key and was safe for now. Amber was glad. She liked Catherine who was a lawyer and bristled with intelligence.

"Suzanne." The woman's flirtatious confidence had slipped a smidge, but now it shone like the sun from behind a cloud. She sauntered over to collect her key, her chin high, her cheek pressed to his. She whispered in his ear and Amber caught every word... she'd make it worth his while. No doubt she would, and no doubt Nathan would lap it up.

Amber's gaze shifted to the four women who remained, separated from the pack, their faces tight in the harsh light, their hands tangled together. Cory prompted them to say their farewells, and it occurred to Amber that Nathan had cut the women most likely to get hurt. They were sensitive and genuine but lacked self-confidence. He was right... they didn't have what it would take to survive multiple key ceremonies and the catfight that was brewing.

The cameras followed the girls en route to their limos, and Amber wandered in their wake. Cassie prompted them to give a brief recap of their experience and their hopes for the future.

Amber listened to their teary disappointment and realised that in the shortest time, Nathan had touched something deep inside each of them. There was an art in that.

The cool night air whispered over her skin, and she rubbed her bare arms. This could work. Already, she'd heard a buzz amongst her staff. There was enormous potential in the footage. The audience would love Nathan. The TV bosses would love her, and she would salvage her career. All would be well, except for the tear-ravaged women who left with their hopes in tatters. It was the risk they took. They had more courage in their glossy fingernails than Amber had in her entire body. Love wasn't for her. No thank you, but if she could help someone else find love, if such a thing existed, well, she could live with that.

The crew lazed around the pool on the aft upper deck with beers in hand, and Amber let the sound of their chatter wash over her. She stood apart from the rest, her arms resting against the railing, her chin on her hands. The lights of Sydney CBD reflected off the black mirror of the harbour and she could hear the soft sigh of the water against the body of the boat. There was the lute-like sound of rigging as it knocked against the mast of a yacht nearby and she could see a ferry in the distance, lit up like a showboat on the water. She was exhausted. It had been one hell of a day and a long night.

She breathed the sweet cool air and savoured the peace of the early morning. She enjoyed the sounds of the team around her, but they needed to get some sleep. They'd be living and breathing the show for the next six weeks. Thankfully, the motor yacht came with a fully fitted out galley, chef, and kitchen staff, along with a captain and crew. She couldn't wait to edit and create the first episode. There was so much excellent footage that she struggled to contain her excitement.

"How did it go tonight? Honestly? Now that it's just you and me."

The sound of Nathan's voice close to her ear was like warm chocolate, dark and rich to her senses. "Oh, it went well, really well. You did an exceptional job," she said with genuine praise. "You played them like a master."

"I'm not sure that's a good thing." He leaned against the handrail and stared moodily into the night.

"Oh, that's an excellent thing for the show. You came across as sensitive, compassionate, and authentic. Every woman in the country will want to share every intimate moment of this journey with you. Your choice of who to send home was inspired. You quickly worked out who didn't have the strength of character to go the distance."

"I liked having your voice in my ear." He leaned in towards her and his shoulder brushed against hers.

Amber stepped back, inviting the cool rush of air to her over-sensitive, over-heated, over-tired body. Her feet hurt, the muscles in her neck were tight, and she longed for a hot shower. "Where's Niko?" She pressed her fingers into her sore neck and tilted her head from one side to the other.

"One of the crew took him for a toilet-run. You look done in."

"It's been a long day."

Nathan stepped in behind her and placed his hands on her shoulders... his warm, strong, provocative hands. And her body contracted. "I'm fine. Thank you. I'll brief you on tomorrow's dates and then we can get some sleep."

"Let me fix this. You have knots upon knots."

His hands worked to release them, and she fought the awkwardness, allowing herself to relax into the oh-that's-so-good for just a moment, but his touch roused memories she didn't want roused and she twisted away from the blistering heat of his hands. "Thanks, truly, but I'm fine."

"These women are important to you, aren't they?" His twilight gaze shone in the dark. "You don't want to see them get hurt, yet by definition, nearly all of them must." He stepped back and leaned against the handrail.

"I know how it feels to get hurt." The lingering warmth of his touch stormed inside her. "I'm sure most of us do."

"I'll be as honest with the girls as I can. I have no desire to go through them like a wrecking ball."

A good analogy. "You'll be the perfect bachelor. Thank you." She took a deep breath and fought the spinning sensation in her head. "Can we talk about the dates tomorrow? I need to go to bed. I'm done in."

"I'll see you at breakfast." He turned his attention to the view. The Opera House and harbour bridge were lit up—stunning against the night sky—as iconic to Australia as the koala and the kangaroo.

Amber walked towards her room and lectured herself with every step. She was almost to the sanctuary of her own space when she was attacked from behind. She went down in a tangle of wet tongue, furry limbs, and doggy breath.

"Niko, Niko, where are you?" Nathan's voice came from the distance.

Amber wrestled with Niko, trying in vain to keep her face away from the lathering of kisses and his enthusiastic clambering. "Niko, get off me." She shoved at him and laughed, but he mistook her defensive moves for engagement and upped his game with a joyous bark. His coat was silky soft, and she couldn't fight the temptation to stroke him as she sought his collar.

"Niko!" The voice came closer. "Oh, I'm sorry Amber..." Nate growled and hauled Niko from her body by the collar. "He has no manners and no finesse when it comes to women."

Amber straightened her top and pushed herself into a seated position. With her hair falling loose from its high ponytail and her skirt too snug to easily get up, she felt bedraggled and exposed. The girl he'd known was inside her still and she didn't want him to recognise her. Puppy eyes. Adoring. Without so much as a whiff of sense.

"Here." He reached out a hand to haul her up from the floor.

"Thank you." She smoothed her skirt down from where it rode up against her legs. She'd always been pale skinned and while her legs were long and shapely, without the help of a tanner, she looked like a corpse. Hence her goth phase. It had been a defensive reaction to the school's stereotype of beauty. With her red-toned hair—she preferred chestnut as a descriptor—dyed black and her skin white, she'd made a statement. Now? She pushed her bottle-blonde hair away from her face and looked down at her bottle-tanned legs, then shifted her gaze to the crazy beat of Niko's tail against the floor. She'd learned it was easier to conform than to resist the tide of public opinion. And success came to those who looked the part, even if they didn't feel it.

"Well, good-night then." Nate's smile raised her blood pressure and left her insides yearning. He reached over to remove a strand of hair from her face just as she reached to fix it herself, and their hands banged awkwardly together.

"Oh." She retracted her hand like she'd been scalded but it

was too late. Time slowed, and what swirled between them was far from cool. His gaze held hers with a magnetism she couldn't fight. It sapped the strength from her limbs, and she had to cling to her professional veneer. "Good-night." She forced the words from her over-tight chest and over-stretched lungs. "And Nathan?" Her gaze dropped from the twilight blue of his eyes to his lips and back again. She felt light-headed as memories of his kisses rose like ghouls, evocative and enamouring.

"Yes?" Niko lunged towards her again, and Nathan adjusted his grip, his gaze communicating with something deep and hungry inside her.

"You have twenty perfectly willing women downstairs. I'm not part of the deal. Are we clear?" Are we clear? She lectured herself in the silence of her own head because, truly, she couldn't disengage herself from the magic he conjured.

"Crystal." He gave her a mischievous, cheeky, impossible-to-resist kind of grin. "But I could have sworn you wanted to kiss me just now."

"You're wrong. I know most women must melt into a puddle of lust at your feet, but I'm not one of them." Not anymore. She hadn't wanted to kiss him. Had she? No. She might have looked at his mouth, because he was a handsome man and his mouth did this quirky thing that pulled at her in a most provocative way, but no, kissing had not crossed her mind until he'd mentioned it, and now that he had, she could think of nothing else.

Amber reached for her door because, frankly, her bones weren't doing their job and if she didn't have something to support her, she might well melt into a puddle of lust at his feet, and there was no way that was going to happen. Ever.

Again. "This is a working relationship and that's the end of it. I don't date people I work with, and where you're concerned, I'd rather not revisit the past."

His gaze was like sunlight drawn to a fiery point and the years fell away until she saw it... her heart raw and bleeding and sacrificed at the altar of Neanderthal Nathan... the gaping wound in her chest. The emptiness. The dark despair. The engulfing shame.

Their history was like ballast, and she had to push through it to breathe.

She'd wanted to kiss him? Oh, hell. She'd wanted to kiss him. Heat flushed her cheeks, and she cursed herself for being so transparent.

He'd wanted to kiss her. She'd seen it in his eyes. The man was a player. Hadn't she just seen him at work, masterfully convincing twenty-four women he was interested in each and every one of them? He conjured a dangerous magic, and she should know better than to play with fire. Fire mesmerised. Fire burned. Fire destroyed. And what was she thinking? He was her lead man. With a bevy of beauties at his beck and call.

"What made you decide you needed a dog the size of a bear?" She sought conversational safe ground and her grip tightened on the door.

"Oh, Niko found me. He was a very hungry and maltreated stray." Nathan's gaze dropped from hers, and he started back along the empty passageway. "Don't worry. He's house-trained now."

"Great." The words hungry and maltreated echoed through her mind. It wasn't the dog she was worried about. Six weeks was an interminably long time to weather the kind of storm that raged inside of her.

Well, batten down the hatches, she lectured herself. No way would she allow that man to take her down twice.

Chapter Three

Two hours later, Amber walked into the large, modern dining area on the upper deck. A massive oval shaped chandelier hung over the enormous table and generous-sized chairs. The sun was bright, and the morning was fresh. She was dressed in jogging gear and needed a glass of water. She was done with trying to sleep. Her mind just couldn't disengage from the thought of Nathan down the hallway in the massive master suite, probably naked, a thought so disturbing she couldn't breathe through the tightly knotted muscles of her diaphragm. Which meant that she wasn't ready for the sight of Nathan—fully dressed in grey track pants which hung criminally low on his hips and a faded red t-shirt which lovingly hugged every impressive curve of his body—returning his breakfast dishes to the side board, where a smorgasbord of food waited in heated bain-maries.

Nathan had a phone pressed to his ear and his voice was gravelly, his tone intimate and reassuring. "I'll call you every day. You know where I am. If you need me, I'll be there." He lowered the phone to the marble counter and jumped in surprise when he realised, he wasn't alone. "Oh, Amber, you're up early."

"Nathan." The word snaked from her mouth like a venomous

serpent from a dark crevice. "Do I need to remind you that lovers—outside the bounds of this vessel—are off limits? You've signed a contract. You're here to find a bride, and I forbid any communication with women from outside."

"You forbid it, do you?" His tone was loaded with all kinds of pitfalls and if a gaze could sharpen to the point of a spear, she'd be in mortal danger.

Amber's stomach seethed with slithering reptiles. "You've signed a contract." Her tone reflected the frustration of a too short, too sleepless night.

"Nowhere in the fine print did it mention sacrificing my soul." He turned away from her, his snarl audible. "Besides, that's a price a man can't pay twice."

"What's that supposed to mean?" Fangs sank into her organs and toxins raced through her veins. "If you're referring to our once-off..." *Hot, hot, hot, sexual encounter* came to mind along with rousing images she'd rather not remember of his tanned and muscled body, and his passionate kisses as they all but devoured each other. "...*Liaison* for which you deserved an Oscar for your acting performance, that's a mistake I won't repeat." She took a deep breath. "You're here to find love and love you will find. On screen. On schedule. As promised. No outside... *liaisons.*"

"I understand that this TV confectionary is important to you." His tone implied he didn't share the sentiment.

No way would she let him know *how* important it was to her.

"And I'm fully aware of my obligations." His eyes turned dark like a storm had blown in, buffeted by hurricane-force winds. "But I've given you my word, and I don't appreciate your lack of faith."

"Fine. You're right. I'm sorry." She reached for a pod to slip into the coffee machine and visibly shook with the effort of trying to control her physical reaction to him. She needed caffeine and fast. "I'm still recovering from Dan's unexpected exit."

"Which reminds me. We need to discuss product placement." He steered her attention to an array of vitamin supplements, powders, and potions with a company logo splashed across them.

He'd taken it upon himself to display his wares. No doubt he'd done the same in the girl's dining area downstairs. "About that…" She paused as the scent of freshly brewed coffee captured her senses and settled the writhing sensation inside of her. "Biovite is one of our major sponsors. It won't be possible to expose your brand without putting that relationship at risk."

"We had an agreement." His words were sharp with annoyance.

"No. There was no agreement. It's not in the fine print." She turned to him. "Nor in the not-so-fine print. Would you like one of these?"

"No, thank you. In my world, a verbal agreement is as binding as a printed one."

Since when, she thought, her memories like a velvet trap. He'd invited her to his final year formal only to take Bethany Wyman when it came to the crunch. "There was no verbal agreement. If I remember correctly, you told me you wanted product placement rather than asking if it was possible. If you'd asked, I could have explained there was a conflict of interest. When did you branch into vitamins and supplements?" She leaned against the counter, her steaming coffee in hand.

"A couple of years ago." He raked his hand through his hair

40

and left it deliciously mussed. "Look, this is important. There must be a way to appease your sponsors and provide exposure for our products."

Amber sipped her coffee and tried to care, but frankly she didn't. "None that I can think of, but John may have some ideas. He's the production designer. He creates the visuals for the show. Maybe when the scenes are offsite, he could manage something, but I'm not confident. We need to go through today's schedule, but until I go for a run, I'm no good to anyone."

"And I'm no good to you without exposure for our products. That was the deal," he said through teeth that were prised together.

"There was no deal. You came to me with a perfectly tied bow if I remember correctly." She gave him a saccharine smile, her mind turning to gift horses and the warnings that came with them.

"I need exposure for our products. It's important. Who's in charge of sponsorship?"

"That would be me," Amber replied. "Biovite is one of our major sponsors. I can't renege on an agreement with the business that's financing the show." She stifled a yawn, then flushed when she realised how rude she must appear.

"Trouble sleeping?"

"Yes." He seemed to stare right into her, and her toes clenched inside her running shoes. "I was wound up about the footage." Liar. She was too wound up about the man she'd almost kissed and even now, she felt an unwanted tug of attraction.

"Do you usually have coffee before you run?" He strode towards the door, loose-limbed and relaxed. "You might want to try one of our green smoothies when you get back." He pointed to the products. "I think you'll find yourself energised in a healthier way."

She didn't usually run after caffeine. What happened to the water she'd come to get? He'd messed with her head, and now he'd messed with her body. She was as wound up as a jumping jack, and her cheeks flushed pink when she realised, he was cucumber cool. "Thanks for caring." She gave him a feigned smile. The only person Neanderthal Nathan cared about was himself. That was a lesson she'd learned a long time ago.

His gaze lingered on her mouth, and she fought the urge to moisten her lips.

"I left a map on the table with all of the running tracks hereabouts." He nodded towards a pamphlet that lay open. I was reading it while I ate my breakfast. "I took Niko down to the foreshore near the Botanic Gardens."

"Trouble sleeping?" Her words were frayed at the edges because her mouth was dry, and her movements were as stiff as a cardboard cut-out. She put the coffee cup down and cussed. Why did she let him get to her?

"Yes, and I think we both know why we couldn't sleep."

"It was a massive day yesterday and a long night. Today will be a big one, too." Her gaze slipped towards his potions. "Do those things really work?"

"Yes, they're exceptional. And Amber?" He paused and her heart rate soared as if her brain was already in flight-mode, but her body hadn't caught up. "I'm sorry for how it turned out back at school. It was never my intention to hurt you. I enjoyed our friendship. It was immature and arrogant of me to be goaded into the bet in the first place. In truth, we connected, and you meant more to me than I made out. In trying to save face, I hurt you and that was wrong."

An apology? She grappled to find her words. "It *was* wrong. On so many levels." She needed her anger. She needed to hate him, because if she didn't hate him, she'd love him and if she loved him? She'd have to stand behind the camera and watch him cavort with the beautiful, glamorous, leggy creatures of perfection she'd hand-picked for that very purpose—she'd created her own personal hell. Oh, the fates must be laughing at her expense. He was out of her league and always would be. "I'll see what I can do about your products, but it won't be easy."

"The smoothies are as good as a balanced meal. Better in some ways." He looked at her as if to assess how genuine her capitulation was. "A large proportion of the profits from these products go towards funding a mental health recovery program for teenagers struggling with depression, eating disorders, and other challenges. Not only that, the business gives those teenagers a job and a sense of purpose, along with self-respect. When the unit's funding was cut, we were able to step in with a self-funded solution. My sister is at the helm, and I want her to succeed."

"Oh." Amber's thoughts scattered like ashes on the ocean. "I see. Well, I'll talk to John, and we'll work something out. There must be a way to meet your obligations and ours."

"And Amber?"

"Yes?" Her body shook from the effects of too much caffeine too early in the morning. It had nothing to do with the intensity of his blue gaze, or the treacherous feelings that stirred inside her. He couldn't know how deeply she'd suffered, or how his behaviour had changed her at a cellular level. She hadn't fit in. She was a scholarship kid, a Wannabe, while most of her peers had wealthy parents who could afford to send their children to private school. They'd met through a chance encounter in Hyde Park. A place she'd liked to retreat to with a book, and a place he'd liked to jog. It had become a thing. He'd stop to chat, and she'd look forward to seeing him.

Nathan was the quintessential privileged, good-looking, arrogant, too-cool-for-school kind of jock... it was a miracle they'd connected at all. And not much had changed from where she was standing. So, he'd apologised. Words were cheap. Especially his. So, he gave money to a charity. Probably for the tax deduction or the kudos he received in the media. And his sister was probably just like him. That didn't mean he actually cared, and as for Niko, he'd saved a stray. So what? Who wouldn't fall for the rambunctious appeal of a puppy? Good. Head cleared. Move on. Go for a run. Now.

"I'm no longer the person you knew back then."

He was still there? Standing in the doorway like he was torn between going and staying. *Go already. Please.*

"Life has a way of teaching us the lessons we need to learn."

Amber's chin dropped to the vicinity of her knees and when he did turn to leave, she was left with the enduring image of his very tight butt, and his tanned, strong, muscular legs.

He was right. Neanderthal Nathan was a lesson learned. Jason Berringer was a lesson learned. She couldn't trust herself around men. That was the guts of it and from this point forward, she'd do as she'd done back in school. She'd focus on her work, make *Bachelor on Board* a brilliant success, and ensure Nathan was safely married. To someone else. And she'd remember to balance her crazy work ethic with rest, so she didn't end up with chronic fatigue syndrome, which post-Nathan had turned her life upside down.

Chapter Four

A mber focused on the metal steps beneath her feet. Another wave of dizziness assailed her, and she lifted her gaze from the moving water below to look up and ahead, but then her gaze snagged on the equally disturbing sight of Nathan's rear not twenty metres ahead of her. It was the perfect antidote to the dizzy sensation that robbed her of her equilibrium whenever she got too high and the Sydney Harbour Bridge was too high in anyone's language. Look at the view, she lectured herself—the Opera House, the city skyline, the water... Amber breathed—deep, long, invigorating breaths. You can do this, she promised herself. You will. Think of Jason. Think of what he stole from you. Get it together. It's okay. You feel fine. You're okay. One step at a time.

She didn't feel fine. She felt awful. Green. Thirsty. She stopped and closed her eyes, visualising solid ground beneath her feet. She grappled with the steel grey and blue coverall to loosen its hold on her throat and longed for water. She took deep draughts of the warm, exhaust-tainted air and, with a final mental shove, opened her eyes and moved forward over the last stretch onto the top of the bridge.

Nathan and Juliette, a lovely brunette who embraced the adventure without breaking a sweat, appeared at ease with each other. Excellent, she lectured herself. Cory introduced the challenge, and she sought the horizon for some sort of equilibrium. Breathe.

"Are you okay?" It was Nathan's voice, gravelly, concerned and too close to her ear. "You're panting and I have to say it's kind of distracting."

Hell, the mic. Nathan would be the death of her, one way or another.

"Thank you, yes." She clamped her teeth together and forced the clutch of panic from her chest. "I'm not a fan of heights, that's all. I'm trying to clear my head." That had to be the understatement of the year.

"Breathe into your belly. And count to ten with long, slow breaths."

She didn't answer, just held on to the railing and closed her eyes, breathing deeply, oblivious to the wind that pulled at her coveralls and ponytail. A wave of nausea left her spinning, and she groaned. Panic fluttered in her chest until strong arms closed around her, and her body rested against a warm, solid chest.

"You're fine, Amber." Nathan's voice was warm and smooth like heated caramel. "This bridge is solid and you're safe. It's been here for decades. I'm guessing it will be here for decades to come."

"Of course, it will." She fought for a tone that was no-nonsense sensible, but the wobble in her voice gave her away. There was a crumbly edge to it like pavlova—a hard and crispy meringue that disappeared into sweet nothingness the moment it hit the tongue. Amber dug deep to find the courage she needed to push him away. She turned—carefully—and saw humour in his sky-blue eyes. "Thank you, but your job is to look after Juliette. Let's get on with the challenge and get off this blasted bridge."

"Absolutely." He grinned, his eyes sparkling. "Are you sure you don't need mouth to mouth resuscitation?"

"I'm fine, thank you." Was that a subtle reference to a kiss? No. No. No. She was not the one he should be kissing. That would be the glamorous, gorgeous, and impatient woman who stood waiting, her hair torn by the wind. "Let's get on with the challenge." Who wouldn't say 'yes please' to lip-locking with Nathan on top of the Sydney Harbour Bridge to break the world record for the longest onscreen kiss?

The Guinness Book of Records' official stood to the side, his timer at the ready.

"Okay, everyone." Amber straightened and kept her gaze on Nathan. "Positions. Juliette, are you ready?"

"Yes, Amber. Just waiting on you." The woman's tone had a sickly-sweet sting. "*And Nathan.*" She gave him a look which suggested she'd like to eat him alive.

"Right." Amber realised Nathan was still hovering, too close for comfort, and gritted her teeth. "Nathan?"

"Are you sure you're alright?" His words were quiet. Just for her.

"I will be. Let's get this over and done with."

Nathan and Juliette faced each other; their hands linked. The Opera House, and the sleek white superyacht that had become their home, were perfectly positioned in the background. The sky was blue and vast, and the sun shone, warm and steady... more steady than Amber who fought to keep the vista in the periphery of her vision, and her focus on the scene in front of her. If she tried hard, she could convince herself she wasn't perched high above the city on a precarious tangle of metal.

The boom operator managed to combat the breeze and kept the microphone near the action, but away from the camera frame. The camera guy glanced towards her with concern. She gave a thumbs-up and called for action.

The standing record of three minutes, forty-eight seconds was an achievable goal, but the four minutes and ten seconds they kissed was the longest four minutes and ten seconds of her life. It was like swallowing a snarling, clawing, flesh-eating cray. Every second was like acid. Every minute like cyanide. She looked away. She schooled herself. But it was Nathan's hands on Juliette's very shapely rear that stole her attention. Not to mention the heat they generated as they tasted, savoured, and devoured each other. For a first kiss, she had to admit, there was a lot of chemistry. Explosive came to mind. This was television at its best. A ticking clock. A beautiful couple and breath-taking scenery. And a kiss. Like none she'd filmed before.

But very like one she'd experienced. That cray she'd swallowed took a pincer-grip on her insides. She'd been so lost in the magic of it, in the wonder and the adoration, she'd believed—fully—that he'd shared her feelings. But what if he hadn't? Of course, he hadn't. Her humiliation reached new depths. If he could kiss a woman he'd just met with this level of enthusiasm, for how long? Her gaze shifted to her watch. Another excruciating minute had passed. Then the kisses she remembered with such sweet agony were nothing more than a fantasy. She felt gutted and strung-out. Overwhelmed and foolish.

Cory egged them on and no doubt, every viewer in Australia would be holding their breath and willing them to break the record. She tore her gaze away to study the intricate metal structure of the harbour bridge. Far below—whoa, she couldn't look down—there were cars. Lots of them. Every colour. And beyond them was the city, the closely packed buildings and the frantic pace that created a hum of sound audible even at this distance. The breeze picked up and tore at her hair. Her coveralls. She took to counting in her head, anything to keep herself from spinning out with the height and definitely not the stress of watching Nathan kiss Juliette. Four minutes and ten seconds was an interminably long time.

Nathan gave Juliette ninety-five percent of his attention which was about his best effort. He knew how to kiss. He knew how to make a woman feel like a goddess. He wanted Juliette to feel special, but his heart wasn't in it. For one, there was Amber in his ear and he could hear the catch in her breath, the jerky intake of air as she struggled to control her fear. He'd forgotten she hated heights, but he hadn't forgotten the sound of that catch in her breath or the sound of her groan or the awkward moment in his teenage enthusiasm when he'd realised, she was a virgin and stopped mid-thrust.

Why hadn't she told him? Why had it mattered? Because she'd deserved better. Over the years, she'd become pristine white to his dark-lord black.

And kissing another woman on national television for what seemed like a lifetime would do nothing to convince her he'd changed. When it came to Amber, he was thwarted at every step like a divine being presided over her or a protective genie.

Besides, he had to marry if he wanted to cut off his step-mother's spending. No way would he let that thieving harlot spend any more of his hard-earned fortune, and if his stupid father died before Nate married? That harlot would own him.

His grandfather's company—and all of the work Nate had done to restore it—would belong to her. The recent discovery had left him in a damn hurry to find a wife. The moment he married, the company would be his, and he could stop the financial bleed. He was done carrying his loser father and his bimbo wife. And when his stepmother discovered her husband was no longer a bottomless pit of money? How long before she dumped him?

Nate's tummy muscles clenched, and he struggled to let go of his anger. He fully blamed his stepmother for his sister's eating disorder. Bella was a teenager when their father left them, and the food going into her body—or not—was about the only thing she could control.

Nathan's father had tried numerous business ventures, all of which had failed. Fortunately, Nathan had inherited his grandfather's smarts and learned from his father's mistakes. His stepmother topped the list. Blonde, beautiful and outgoing, she was expensive to run. She liked the finer things in life and expected them. On the other hand, she didn't much like to work. His father was blind and senseless when it came to his wife.

Nathan refocused his attention on the woman in his arms.

She could kiss, and she knew how to melt against a man with provocative invitation, albeit with a man she barely knew. Not a hardship for her if she was anything like his stepmother. His bimbo-barometer had become more sensitive in recent years, and if he wasn't mistaken, it was dollar signs she saw in his eyes rather than anything more substantial.

He needed a wife, but he didn't need a financial encumbrance. If he had to marry, and he did, then he wanted a woman who could stand on her own two feet and that's when he heard the slight sob in his ear. Amber. His heart lurched, and he schooled himself to keep kissing, to pay attention, but his focus was on every small sound emitted from his earpiece. Was she okay?

Cory started the count down, and he felt nothing but relief. Juliette was a beautiful woman, and she kissed like a siren, so he should have enjoyed every indulgent moment. Why wasn't he? And then the record was done, but still they kissed. He could hear the celebratory sounds, but they had to nail this thing with time to spare. He wanted the show to be a success—it was an interesting thought. Another minute at least, but the catches in Amber's breath stole his attention, and he lifted his head, breaking the intimate connection.

Juliette smiled up at him, and he had to smile back. They were on national television and they'd broken a world record. A magnum of champagne was thrust into his hands, and he poured the soft, fizzy liquid into flutes for them both to share. He saluted Juliette with his glass, and she flushed a delightful pink. Surely, with a smorgasbord of willing women on offer, he could find a wife. He wasn't looking for love. He was looking for compatibility, an intellectual equal, and a signed prenuptial agreement. The woman who gazed up at him so hopefully might be the one. He'd know more after their one-on-one soiree.

"Cut." He heard the relief in Amber's voice and turned to observe her. For a woman who hated heights and who'd no doubt battled her fear the entire climb, she appeared in control. But he'd heard the barely audible whispers. *You've got this. Breathe.* And he felt something shift in his chest. She was brave, and she had courage in spades, but he sensed her vulnerability under the polished, efficient facade, and he promised himself then and there that he'd make this show a success. He owed her.

"What would *your* perfect date look like?" Nathan shifted his attention from his sandwich to the woman who stood beside him in the plush upper deck lounge. The break was a short one. He was formally dressed in black pants and a white shirt, ready for another key ceremony, unlike Amber who was more casually dressed in white skinny jeans and a loose top.

"A picnic on an isolated beach." Her tone was wistful, her voice quiet and low and just for him. "With surf and squeaky white sand and rocks to climb. Shells to find. And wilderness all around. Then a fire on the beach as the sun sets, with freshly caught fish in foil followed by toasted marshmallows. And definitely champagne. Isolation and privacy."

"Sounds blissful. Is that on my date list?"

"Maybe. Once we're down to six ladies or so, and we get to Broome."

"Intriguing." The idea of a date with Amber settled in his mind and took root. "Today was great. Except for the fact that you were terrified the whole time. You couldn't have delegated the climb to one of your minions?"

"I'm very protective of my intellectual property since, well, let's just say someone I trusted stole my idea for a TV series and sold it as his own." She eyed him over the rim of her coffee cup. "I plan to be very hands-on with this production."

"A colleague? Someone you dated?"

"Yes." Her gaze broke away from his and settled on something behind him. "On both counts." Her cheeks flushed pink, and he readily saw the tension in her jaw and the rigidity in her spine.

"Well he didn't deserve you." Nate hadn't deserved her either.

"Do you have someone in your life now?" He couldn't help but ask. He had no right, but he had to know if she had a man somewhere, waiting impatiently in the wings for *Bachelor on Board* to be ticked off her to-do list. The thought was like thick Turkish coffee. Bitter and difficult to digest. He enjoyed their moments of quiet. She was the calm in the eye of the storm, the steady in the midst of the crazy. And crazy was what half of these women had already become, trapped together with nothing to do except discuss their hopes and feelings for him, blowing everything out of proportion. No doubt the close quarters on the boat were designed with that purpose in mind.

"Not at the moment." Her gaze flicked away from his.

Relief washed through him like a warm wave, relaxing every tight muscle in its path. Cassie chose that moment to interrupt them. She shoved a clipboard towards Amber.

Amber glanced over it and, with a brief apology, turned and walked towards one of the lighting specialists. She was efficient and ran the show like a well-oiled machine. Her staff respected her and not once had he heard her raise her voice. He'd seen the looks a couple of the film crew gave her. Admiration. Sexual interest, too, if he wasn't being paranoid, but she appeared oblivious to their glances.

He had a better understanding now of why she kept to herself. Not in a rude way and it wasn't like any of them had much energy for carousing by the end of the interminably long days of filming, but she maintained a distance. He observed her as she worked and noted the dark smudges under her eyes. Their schedule was hectic, and *he* was tired. He hated to think how tired she must feel. Amber finally returned with two fresh coffees in hand, and he took his gratefully.

"Do you still live in Sydney?" he asked as she leaned back

against the railing to take a sip from hers.

"Yes. After high school I stayed on to go to University and now, for work."

"And your family? Are they still in Tasmania?" He vaguely remembered their conversations all those years ago before he'd taken their connection to a sexual level. His mates had found out about their rendezvous in the park, and laid down the mantle, mocking him that he could never bone someone as brainy and outside the square as Morticia Reed. His teenage brain had turned to the prize. What he hadn't anticipated was how impossible to resist she'd become with every provocative opinion she'd shared, and what had started out as a challenge had become his yard stick. No woman had piqued his interest in quite the same way since.

"Yes. They're synonymous with the small town where I grew up. Anything that happens outside their small world doesn't much interest them."

"Are you serious? Don't they know what you've achieved?"

"Not enough to convince them I'm not wasting my time. They're waiting for me to get it out of my system and come home. My mum believes a woman's place is in the kitchen. Besides, they don't even own a television. What about yours? They were going through a difficult time back then. Did they work it out?"

"No. My dad married the woman he was cavorting with. She's maybe five years older than me, and they live on the waterfront in Manly. My mum and sister live in Coogee, and I have an apartment in Darling Harbour. I like to be close to my office."

"Oh, no. I'm sorry. I remember how worried you were at the time." Her green eyes captured his and he felt her compassion wrap around him like a hug.

"You got your MBA though, like you hoped," she said more brightly. "And your CV suggests you've been highly successful."

"I like to work." Work gave his life meaning. Work filled in the empty spaces that echoed inside of him. Spaces that seemed to have filled since he'd come on board. Perhaps a relationship was what he needed after all. Perhaps he was lonely. Perhaps Dan was right.

"That's good because we have about five minutes until we need to get back on set. Just enough time to hit the bathroom." She reached for his empty cup. "How's Niko liking his temporary home?"

"He's loving all the attention, and the crew are clamouring to take him for a run. I'd like to see how the girls react to him. I want a woman who isn't too much of a princess to get down and rumble with him. Perhaps he could accidently escape onto the lower deck. I'd love to see their reactions."

"That would certainly create some madcap footage." She laughed and the sound appealed to him more than it should have. "Okay. That could work. Oh, and I've spoken with the powers that be about your product placement. Off-site we have some scope and it's a definite yes for the home visits. On board the ship, our hands are tied."

"That will have to do." His gaze sought hers. "Thank you. I appreciate it."

"No problem." She smiled a smile he felt all the way to his cramped toes and bustled off, one of the camera crew capturing her attention within moments with an earnest question.

Key ceremony two tonight, he thought, and he'd select another woman to leave the ship. Then there would be nineteen on the cruise to Brisbane. So far, he was finding it very easy to let them go. Their true colours were beginning to appear, and he had little patience for jealous catfights.

The sun was dropping over Brisbane city when Nick found Amber sitting on the aft sun deck dressed in cut-off denim shorts and a singlet top, her hair pulled back in a high ponytail, eating café style buttery raisin toast and sipping what smelled like peppermint tea. Niko lazed against her, his head on her lap. The scent of cinnamon and spice made Nate's mouth water.

"Hi." He stepped into the adjacent dining area and over to the sideboard where he selected an empty glass and reached for his green superfood powder. He measured a small amount before adding water. With the harried pace of eating on the run, he was grateful for the fast fix. "Would you like one of these?"

"No, thanks. I had one this morning though. It even tasted good." There was surprise in her tone and admiration. "I think you're onto a winner with those."

"I know I am." They'd kept his sister alive, even if he'd had to force feed her, sip by sip.

"We need to brainstorm your next two dates. We have the group date sorted out, but who would you like to take with you for the next one-on-one?"

"Catherine, I think." He settled himself into the seat opposite her. Niko opened one eye then closed it again, making no effort to move away. Interesting. "She seems more grounded than the rest. Intelligent and sensible." It was dark outside, but the lights from buildings along the Brisbane River twinkled and reflected across the water.

"Did you enjoy your adventure today?"

"Jumping out of a plane with a woman sure stymies first-date awkwardness." His stomach had churned, and he'd held on tightly to Rebecca's hand to stop the shaking. Hers had trembled in his and there had been camaraderie in the shared experience. But with the cameras on them, they'd had little choice but to embrace it.

Still, his fear had nearly choked him when he'd thought of his sister and what would happen to her if he wasn't around to keep her safe... standing at the door in his harness with his instructor, Gerry, had been one of the longest moments of his life.

"Rebecca was incredibly brave, and the view of Brisbane was amazing." Once he'd gotten over the throat-grabbing pull of the wind and the sensory overload that was so intense he really didn't remember much of the freefall part of the dive. It happened so quickly it was like his brain couldn't catch up. "Once the parachute went up, there was the most incredible sense of freedom, and seeing the land come up towards us was phenomenal. I couldn't believe it when we touched down on the beach in one piece."

"There's no way I could have done that." Her face paled at the thought, and he remembered her dislike of heights.

"I'm not sure jumping out of a plane is on everyone's wish list. To be honest, I wasn't sure about it myself."

Amber took a sip of her tea and stroked Niko's head. "I didn't breathe easily until you were both back on solid ground. It might make for sensational television, but I was terrified of everything that could go wrong."

"You were worried about me?" He shot her a facetious grin.

"*And* Rebecca," she pointed out. "Besides, I can't afford to lose another bachelor."

He loved the way he could ruffle her composure. She

presented such a polished front to the world, and he was sure she didn't realise how often she reassured herself, just under her breath. *You're okay. You can do this.* The whispered words had echoed in his mind on the verge of his first skydiving attempt. He couldn't show fear. Not on national television. Not when Rebecca appeared animated and excited beside him. Besides, the thought of Amber waiting on the ground was enough to make him follow Rebecca out of the plane. Ladies first wasn't quite as gallant at twelve thousand feet.

"Rebecca earned her key, that's for sure." He enjoyed these quiet moments when it was just the two of them—well, three of them if he counted his very contented pooch.

"You appeared relaxed together over lunch." They'd set up on the forward deck, a lounge area that doubled as a helipad. "Sparks flew between you. Do you think she might be the one?"

"Rebecca is good company, and she has a wicked sense of humour."

Something sharp flashed into Amber's eyes and if he hadn't known better, he'd have thought it was jealousy. But no. There was nothing to see now. Nothing but professional interest. Cool and calm.

"But chemistry only gets a relationship so far."

"What else are you looking for?" Amber stroked Niko's ears and her gaze pulled away.

"I want someone whose companionship I can enjoy. Sparks are like fireworks. They burn bright in the short-term, but they're quickly gone. I'm looking for compatibility and a signed prenuptial agreement."

"That sounds very cynical. What happened to the playboy squillionaire of magazine fame who always has a glamour-puss of one variety or another on his arm?"

"You, of all people, should understand the power of the press." His voice was quiet. "I rarely date a woman more than once or twice, and those pictures were taken at charity events where a partner is a requirement. Besides, the publicity helps generate funds and people see what they want to see. I prefer to focus on business."

"Why the short expiry date?" She observed him over the rim of her cup, her green gaze steady. "In high school, there were lots of girls to get through, I understand that, but you're twenty-eight and you must be ready for something more meaningful, or why would you have come on the show?"

"Like love, you mean?"

"Yes. A special someone to share your life with."

"I don't believe in love." The words were a mistake, and he knew it the moment they were out of his mouth.

Amber's eyes narrowed. "Then why are you going through the farce of looking for love on this show?" Her tone was sharp enough to cut. She lowered her cup and the liquid sloshed into the saucer. "If you don't believe in it, the television audience won't believe in it, and this show will sink faster than we can make it back to Sydney."

"I need a wife, and this route seemed as valid as any other. Besides, it's a win-win. For Dan. For you." His face flushed, and he forced treacle into his tone. "I owe you." He saw the resistance in her spine, the choking indignation, and he tried for jovial. "Besides, I'm getting to tick a lot of boxes on my bucket list. I've always wanted to try skydiving, and this boat is a treat."

"Do you think your cynicism is rooted in your father's hurtful behaviour? Do I need to organise a counsellor?"

"My father is a great role-model for what *not* to do and how *not* to turn out. I was fully on the same path as him. Girls fell at my feet and sex came easily." He saw her wince, and he would have done anything to back pedal and word that differently. "Not that there weren't moments of significant connection, but generally I was young and foolish, and more concerned about my reputation with my mates than with the girls I dated." He swallowed against the constriction in his throat. It was a miracle she hadn't rejected him on sight. He wouldn't have blamed her. He rested his elbows on the table. "It was only when I saw how much my father's behaviour hurt my mother that I began to realise it wasn't a game. And then…"

Should he let on how badly he'd behaved? She'd already warned him to back off. It wasn't like she wanted to take this any further. They were colleagues. This was a professional relationship. She was safe-ground except for that almost-kiss, which maybe he'd imagined. He'd take whatever he could get and be grateful. He'd treated her badly. Worse than badly. And he'd learned a long time ago that there were some things you couldn't take back, no matter how much you wanted to.

"Do you remember Bethany Wyman from school?"

"How could I forget her?" Amber's tone was carefully casual, but there was pain behind it. She stroked Niko's back with long, smooth strokes and Niko's gaze settled on Nate, brows lifted, as if he'd followed the conversation and couldn't believe Nate's stupidity.

"Yes, of course." Nate should probably apologise for that, too, but there was only so much apologising he could do. He'd behaved badly and with hindsight there was little he could do to fix it. "She overheard us talking about the bet we'd made, and no doubt rushed to share that little tidbit with you. She was jealous of you and determined to get her claws into me. In

60

hindsight, I was very careless and insensitive."

Amber's hand stopped mid-stroke. "I hated her."

If anyone had asked him if a dog could purr, he would have argued the point, but there was a rhythm to Niko's soft grunts that sounded suspiciously like a purr.

"She started night-clubbing and drinking and fell in with a bad crowd. She died on the dancefloor from a drug overdose… and my behaviour contributed to that."

"You were young."

"I was arrogant, and she was manipulative, but she didn't deserve to die. If I'd handled the situation differently, if I'd been more compassionate, more considerate, maybe she'd be alive today."

"That's sad," Amber reflected. "But it was hardly your fault. You were still a child in many ways."

"Well, after Grammar, I grew up quickly." He drained his glass and got to his feet.

If he stayed, there was every risk he'd talk about what else had happened, and he wasn't ready to share it. Not all of it. She didn't need to know the full extent of the burden he carried. Nor did he deserve the relief that would come from sharing it. But she had a right to understand why she'd been treated the way she had. It was enough. "I'll see you in the morning. Would you like me to take your friend there? I can tell you, he's not an easy bed mate. He takes up most of the bed and snores like a freight train."

"Niko." She shook him and he opened one baleful eye. "Bedtime. Your dad is on his way, and so are you."

"Bad luck, mate. How about a quick toilet run before bed?"

At the word, "run", Niko opened both eyes and jerked to his feet. He gave Amber one last lick and high-tailed it across the room, his tail wagging fast enough to get his whole body in on the act.

"Good-night." Nate grinned as Niko tried to squeeze through the doorway at the same time as he did. "Sleep tight." Nate's gaze found Amber's and the connection nearly shattered his resolve to leave. He wrestled Niko into the elevator, and they rode it down to the beach club where they took the gangway onto the dock. Nate welcomed the cool night air, his body heated and antsy. He tucked his hands into his pockets and listened to the soft slap of the water against the sea wall. They strolled along, stopping at every post for Niko to sniff and pee. The night was clear, and the stars shone above.

Nate waited for the familiar feeling of despondency to wash through him, the sense of aloneness that assailed him at this time of night, but it didn't come. Instead, he thought of Amber and her hand on Niko's head, and a wave of warmth rippled through him, bringing a small smile to his lips.

Chapter Five

Nate led Catherine towards the railing at the rear of the luxury motor cruiser they'd commandeered for the afternoon. She felt slender and vulnerable in his arms. They watched the city lights slide by as the vessel headed back along the Brisbane River towards the Portside Wharf Precinct and Cruise Terminal. Their individual date had been exceptional. They'd found a private cove and had spent the afternoon swimming in the water and walking along the beach. He eased back and observed her in the soft light of the tea-lights dotted around in glass lanterns. They'd finished an exquisite meal on the open deck, and he found himself warming to the idea of a future with her. She was leaps and bounds ahead of the rest of the women, and she was capable of a conversation, which was a bonus.

With the magical backdrop and the warm gentle breeze, he found his head inclining towards her. Perhaps it was the champagne, or the lovely afternoon they'd shared on the bay, or maybe it was the hope in the deep chocolate of her eyes and the intensity of her focus... on him... on learning more about him. She was interested. She was interesting. They had a connection. Their lips met, and his eyes closed to better savour the moment, but Amber's breath caught in his ear, and his insides tangled. Hell.

He lifted his lips from Catherine's. Her dark-chocolate eyes appeared glazed as if she'd forgotten where she was. He felt warmth and a connection of sorts, and that would have to do for now. There were too many barriers, too many scars... too many people around them. He reached into his pocket and found the waiting key.

"Catherine. Will you accept this key?" Guilt darkened the edge of his vision. For the show to succeed, he had to woo these women on national television... in front of Amber, yet knowing she was there, in the darkness, distracted him. He wasn't the show pony Amber needed him to be, nor was he the man Catherine needed him to be.

He had to keep his eye on the prize. He wanted his stepmother to watch this show and sweat. He wanted her to worry. He wanted her to know that her plush, comfortable, rort of an existence was coming to an end. An interminably slow demise... one episode at a time. He fully planned to protect what was his and cauterise the bleed.

"Yes, I will." Her voice was soft and intimate. "Thank you." The wistfulness in her tone conjured all kinds of crazy feelings inside him. There was power in it. A power that wrapped around him like a gossamer bind, blissfully gentle, yet steely strong.

The knowing loosened its potency. He would not, could not allow himself to fall for the romantic fiction Amber had created with her incredible attention to detail. Who wouldn't find themselves lured into romance by the perfectly staged scene around him? The slow glide of the boat through the water was soothing and calm, and the air was balmy and warm against his skin.

The lights of the cameras were behind them, and for a moment he could let his face relax. The experience was surreal. He had his arm around a beautiful woman and with the soft sound of the water against the hull and the night wrapped around them, he felt the pull of desire. But it was giving him mixed messages. He had Amber in his ear, in his head, in his heart, and Catherine in his arms. She was beautiful. She deserved to be adored. And he'd enjoyed her company. But thanks to Amber, he felt like a fish in a fishbowl, and his thoughts were in a spin, like he'd spent the day swimming around in circles.

And then Amber's voice sounded in his ear. "Could you turn towards Catherine a bit more? Maybe cup her face with your hands? We can't see you."

"I'm not a puppet." He didn't need Amber's help to seduce a woman. Nor did he want it. Not when his feelings for Catherine were whitewashed by everything he felt for Amber. Not when the feel of Amber's siren-green gaze on him, or the glow of her approval warmed him right through to his bones.

"Sorry?" Catherine looked confused. It wasn't Catherine's fault he felt frustrated. This theatre made a mockery of his feelings. He was flesh and blood, and whilst he had good motives for being on the show—motives he needed to keep front and centre—he would not allow himself to be manipulated by the clichéd romance of these dates. It was like overdosing on sugar until it tasted bitter. Every moment with these women was fictional, and every soft glance Catherine shared with him was delusional. He had to keep it all straight in his mind. He was losing traction on what was real and what was fantasy. He was falling for the fairy-tale wonderment of the tea-lights, the glamour, the gloss.

He was here to find a wife. *Not* to fall in love. *Not* to lose his heart. *Not* to make a fool of himself on national television. Every single one of these contestants had a reason for being here, and he doubted finding love was at the top of the list. A rich husband, maybe. Or a job in modelling, or television?

The boom microphone was a black burr in the periphery of his vision.

He looked into the shadowed depths of Catherine's eyes. "Thank you for a lovely day." She'd done nothing to deserve his rudeness or lack of respect. She'd put herself out there in the public eye and appeared hopeful of winning his heart.

"Thank you, too."

Her smile was honey sweet. Dreams and wishes danced in her eyes, and he took her face in his hands, not because Amber demanded it, but because Catherine looked at him with such trust and longing. "You have a beautiful heart," he whispered.

Tears pooled in her eyes like diamonds. He'd learned a lot about her over the past few hours, and the protector inside of him bristled at the childhood suffering she'd shared. No child should be told they were too stupid to live. Dyslexia was a real hardship, but it wasn't indicative of a child's intelligence. Hadn't Einstein been dyslexic? Catherine had succeeded where many would have failed, and he admired her enormously for that.

"You deserve the *very* best. You deserve to find true love with a man who can give you his heart and his soul." But was Nate that man?

If Catherine knew the man he'd been, she wouldn't want him. Nor would she want the man he'd become. Sure, he was attracted to Catherine physically—he was a virulent man in the prime of his life—that part was easy. Sure, he found her conversation stimulating and interesting. But what if beneath it all he was just like his father? What if his kind of love was less until-death-do-us-part, and more until-the-next-desirable-woman-crosses-my-path? What kind of promise was that anyway? He could only promise his love for now. And right now, he wanted to give this gorgeous woman the special moment she deserved. He lowered his mouth to hers and explored the chemistry that was there between them.

"Cut." Amber's voice was sharp in his ear, but he kept on kissing. This wasn't about Amber. This was about his mission to find a wife, and if he wanted to see if a woman tasted as good as she looked, well, he'd take his time doing it. When he lifted his mouth from Catherine's, she smiled and her soft, full lips brushed against his. Magnetic. Okay. So, she tasted quite nice and they had a connection. It was more than he'd hoped for.

"Let's get back to the mothership. The women are waiting and it's getting late." Amber's voice was edgy. "We're at the wharf."

Nate helped Catherine collect her things. "It was a good afternoon and evening," he assured her. "I really enjoyed your company."

"I enjoyed yours, too." Her eyes flashed in the darkness. "It was great having you all to myself and getting to know you better."

Another key ceremony. Another girl gone. And then there were fourteen. Nate woke to the sensation of movement and the dull drone of the engines. He opened the doors out to the balcony and breathed in the warm, salty air. Water splashed against the side of the hull and the dimpled surface of the water stretched all the way to the horizon, the sun sparkling on the shifting planes.

The group date was a cooking lesson in the stainless-steel galley, and he really enjoyed the banter and the laughter, conscious as always of Amber's proximity. She'd retreated into professional mode since his date with Catherine, and he felt torn. Torn between wanting to please her by finding a contestant he could marry, and wanting *her*, which was madness because after how he'd treated her in the past, she would likely never forgive him.

He understood. He got it. He just didn't like it.

His individual date—with Genevieve—was a candle-lit jacuzzi soak and dinner for two on the upper deck, with lanterns strung above them, and the wide-open night sky packed full of stars. The jacuzzi was fraught given the woman's adventurous touch beneath the foaming bubbles, and at dinner she was too loud, too flirtatious, and too much. Maybe she'd had too much to drink. An abundance of alcohol seemed to accompany his dates.

Cassie had warned him that some of the women were lively, which was perhaps a kind way of saying look-out. Genevieve could stir up trouble with a flick of her false eyelashes, and whilst that worked well for television ratings, it didn't work well in a life-long companion. On the bright side, he'd have no trouble deciding who to cut at the next key ceremony, unless he was forced to keep her on board because of her provocative value.

Afterwards, he found Amber on the aft upper deck watching over Niko as he ran around in the moonlight. She was in loose yoga pants and a fitted top, her feet bare, and her hair pulled back into a ponytail. Her top hugged her slender waist and muscular frame, and the line of her neck was just fine. She worked out. Every morning, no matter how late filming went the night before.

"Fourteen girls left".

"Yes." Her answer was short, and he sensed her anger from the sharpness of her movements.

"What is it?"

"Nothing. The footage is good. Better than good. You're doing a great job." She wrapped her arms around her body.

"So why are you out here with Niko instead of sharing a beer with the crew?"

"I didn't feel like socialising, and Niko was running around causing havoc. It was a win-win."

"It's a win for me, because now I have you all to myself." And he meant it. He loved the connection he sensed with her. They felt like a team. She had his back, and he had hers. The more dates she engineered, the more he realised she knew him. The moments she created roused him and while the leading lady might vary, the woman behind the scenes didn't. She'd become a part of the way he thought. Her voice was there, soothing and reassuring. Perhaps they could move forward. Away from the hurt and the drama of the past.

"It's been a big day. I'll leave Niko to you." She turned away, but he saw the sparkle of tears in her eyes.

"What is it? What's wrong?" He placed his hands on her shoulders—so tense—and turned her towards him, but she pushed him away, and did her best to cover up the emotion that welled there.

"It's nothing. I'm fine." Her body was rigid with the falsehood.

"So why the tears?"

"It's personal." She swiped at the tell-tale moisture.

"I thought we were friends." He studied her face. She was pale and drawn. "Of a kind. Why don't you tell me about it? Maybe talking will help."

Her gaze lifted to his and he saw the battle she fought. Should she stay or should she go? She didn't trust him. Not yet, but their history ran deep and the fact that she was still there, wanting to stay, wanting to go, was more than he deserved.

And then she spoke, her voice raw and quiet. "My grandma is dying. She's ninety-eight. She's been unwell for a while, and it's time for her to go." Her voice hitched and a fresh wave of tears sparkled in her eyes. "I've said my goodbyes—over the phone, but... I won't get to see her again."

He pulled her into his arms and hugged her close. She resisted him at first, her muscles tense, her body rigid, but he felt the stiffness in her soften, and her tears turned to weeping, and her weeping to hard sobs. "You'd like to see her to say goodbye properly."

She nodded against him. "But I can't." She jerked in his arms and he felt rather than heard the sob in her throat. "The shooting schedule's too full. I can't get there and back in time and besides, we're in the middle of nowhere. She has hours to live rather than days."

"So, I'll take you to see her. I can have us back by midday tomorrow. The shoot can wait until then. We'll meet the yacht when it docks at Airlie Beach."

She looked up at him, her eyes swollen, her eye makeup blotchy below her saturated lashes, and his heart stopped. Just like that. And when it started again, it raced with hers. The same rhythm, rapid and steady. For her. With her.

He cared about her? He cared about his sister. He cared

about his mother. Caring he could do. Caring he understood. "We'll go soon. Do you want to get changed?"

"We can't just go. It'll take hours to get to a port. To find a flight. To book it. To hire a car. Tasmania is not like Sydney. It closes at night. But thank you." She swiped at her eyes and made the black smudges worse. He took out his handkerchief and wiped the mess away. Her gaze connected with his and he felt it like a punch to the chest. "We have a group date in the Whitsundays at two o'clock tomorrow, and I need to work on the next individual date and get everything booked. It doesn't just happen. I know it might feel like it does."

"So, leave it to Cassie. We'll work out the details on the way over, and you can call with instructions. I'm sure you have some ideas already sketched out. I can have my chopper here within the hour, and we can be in Tassie in five hours or so. In Lilydale, yes? I'll take you. We'll need to refuel on the way over. There's a helipad on the sun deck. The pilot will find us, and he can stay here while we're gone."

"Yes, but… truly? We could do that? And be back in time?" He heard the fragile thread of hope, the doubtful joy, the longing in her voice.

"Consider it done. You get cleaned up, and I'll see you out here in an hour or so."

She gave him a quick kiss on the cheek. "Thank you." Her gaze clung to his, before she spun away and rushed towards her cabin. He stood there for a half-moment, transfixed. What the hell had just happened?

He took his phone from his pocket and called his co-pilot. The chopper was in a hanger on the roof of his office building—there were some perks to owning the entire block. With a few words and a thank you, it was organised and done.

71

He called Niko and turned to go inside himself. He needed a drink and a bite to eat. It was going to be a long night.

Amber eyed the glossy black shine of the helicopter. He owned it? Of course, he did. He came from money. Her bachelor was seriously wealthy, seriously gorgeous, and seriously out of her league. And her job was to find him a wife. Tears welled in her eyes, and she told herself it was because her precious Grammy was dying and not because Nathan was as far out of reach as ever. She would miss her grammy, and her love for the older woman was an ache that spread from her throat to her heart to the age-old scars that resided there courtesy of Nathan. So maybe he'd changed. Or maybe he felt guilty enough to offer his help. Either way, she was grateful. Very. He couldn't know how much this meant to her. Or how much she appreciated the gesture. That's what this was about. Appreciation. That explained the warmth that spread from her heart to the tips of her toes when she turned, and he was there, handsome in black, his smile a reassuring comfort.

He escorted her towards their ride, his hand resting on the small of her back.

"All set?" He leaned across to check her seatbelt. He had a headset over his ears with a microphone in front of his mouth. He settled a set over her ears, too, and she felt absurdly cosseted. "They help block out the noise so we can talk in peace."

Amber had long-ago learned that the only person she could rely on was herself. It was odd to allow a man to take charge. She looked out of the window, and beyond the lights of the boat it was dark. Mile upon mile of open water. How dangerous was it to fly this contraption with no visibility? Anxiety warred with her need to see her grammy one last time. Fear sat cold and clammy on her skin. They had to fly over land and sea and navigate the trees and hills... they'd have to land on the local football ground. How could they do all of that in the dark? What if they got lost? The landmarks would be shadows in the night.

"Don't worry. I know what I'm doing." Nate's voice was calm. "You're okay. You can do this."

How did he know her mantra? His words mirrored the ones she muttered to herself over and over whenever worry wormed its way into her thoughts. Which was often. Had she said them aloud, forgetting her voice would sound in his ear? What else had been captured by the mic? Shame washed away on a wave of panic as the machine lifted off the ground, straight up into the dark void of the night. She stiffened with the unfamiliar sensation, and her breath must have caught for Nate reached across and took her hand in his, comforting and strong. The rigor mortis in her bones eased, and the air jammed in her lungs found its way free.

"It's okay, Am. You're fine." His gravelly tone stirred something deep in her chest, and she squirmed with the sensation. It was like she was a marionette, and he'd pulled strings she didn't know existed. Heart strings? She'd never understood the term, but that was what it felt like... like he'd pulled at her heart, and she'd felt it respond.

"It's okay. We're okay." She clung to the warmth of his hand. "We are."

She opened her eyes—they'd been closed? —and saw his handsome face illuminated by the lights from the dash. Warmth rushed to her chest, and she felt overwhelmed. Overwhelmed by the strength of her feelings. Feelings that should have died a long time ago, buried by her shame. Feelings too big, too loud, too raw to revive. Don't do it. Don't soften, she schooled herself. He couldn't be trusted. He was a shark in the ocean. A snake in the grass. Never again. Her heart had toughened and grown a protective shell, hiding what was precious inside. Her hopes. Her dreams. Her desires… She kept them close and safe. She stood alone. But right now, it felt good to know she wasn't alone. Nathan squeezed her hand, and the tears she'd held at bay fell hot against her cheeks.

Her thoughts turned to her grandma. "Go," her grammy had whispered. "Go and find yourself. Explore the world. You're too big for this town. Life has grand plans for you." The words had kept her moving forward despite her fears. She'd taken every opportunity and faced down her family's resistance because Grammy was there, reassuring her, encouraging her, promising her that all would be well.

Now it was her turn to do the same for Grammy and, thanks to Nathan, she could. She prayed they would get there in time. She wanted—needed—to say goodbye. To see Grammy, to hug her, to thank her. To promise that all would be well.

She'd helped Amber hold her head high. "You've done nothing to be ashamed of," she'd soothed. "You gave your love to someone who didn't deserve it. That's how we learn. We make mistakes. The shame is *his*, my darling, not yours."

Hours later, they landed in Lilydale on the oddly familiar dark splotch of ground that was the football oval. The noise of the rotors died and there was silence. Stars sparkled in the blackness, as thick as a snowstorm—so many compared with the city. Nathan helped Amber out and when her feet touched the earth, she embraced him, her emotions as scattered as the planets above. "Thank you," she whispered. "Thank you."

"You're welcome." His lips settled on her forehead, soft and warm and honey sweet. She lifted her gaze to his, but it was too dark and too shadowy to see what swam in his eyes. But whatever it was swam in the air between them, too, and it took some moments to break the pull of it. To step back and walk and take the lead.

The house was an easy fifteen-minute stroll from the oval and she could see it on the hill, the lights from the front room, a welcoming beacon. It was late, but her family were awake. She'd called ahead and her fears near tripped her as she hurried over the uneven ground. She jumped when she heard a scuttle in the vegetation, and she couldn't quite stifle the scream. Nathan reached out for her hand and she savoured the strength in his grip—the warmth that seeped into her heart. Later, she'd distance herself from the comfort he gave, but for now, she took what was on offer and was grateful for it.

"Nearly there." Her breath came hard and fast with the steep rise of the hill. "Just ahead. You can see the light." His grip tightened on hers, and she squeezed back. Never in a million years would she have envisaged Nathan in Lilydale. Not here where her country girl heart was exposed. But he was here and that was the guts of it. She hurried up to the old-fashioned metal gate and pulled it open with a yank. The gate clanged shut behind them, and their steps sounded against the concrete path. The front door opened before they reached it and a voice called out across the veranda. "Is that you, Am?"

"Yes, Dad. It's me." She forced calm into her tone. "I'm sorry for the late hour."

"Grammy has been asking for you. Thank God you're here."

"Thank Nathan I'm here." She climbed the final steps and fell into her father's arms. She held on and breathed him in, his familiar scent easing the tightness and the flurry inside her.

There was no place that felt so good. But then she remembered her manners and pulled back. "Dad, this is Nathan Moretti. Nathan, this is my dad, Joe."

"Hi, Joe." Nate extended his hand. "I'm sorry, sir, to be here under such sad circumstances."

"Yes, young man, we're all sorry for them, but my mother has had a full and happy life, and she's ready to go. She's just hanging on now, waiting for my girl here to say her goodbyes. I thank you for making that possible."

Amber stifled a sob and allowed her father to take her back into the comfort of his arms. "Is she awake?"

"As much as she can be. She's dosed up on medication. She sleeps a lot, but she's having a mouthful of puree as we speak. They told us to withhold food, but no person should have to suffer like that. Her time will come and when it does, we'll be with her."

"Yes," Amber agreed. "Dad, could you please get Nathan a drink, while I go and see Grammy."

"She's in her room, love."

"Grammy?" Amber whispered, standing at the threshold, yearning yet afraid. The familiar scent of lavender washed over her.

"Come in, Am." It was her mum's voice from the semi-dark, the soft glow of a lamp revealing a crocheted blanket tucked around her grammy in the bed. "I'm so glad you're here." She rose and gave her a quick hug, before backing towards the door. "Grammy's been asking for you. Over and over."

"It's okay, Grammy. I'm here." Amber settled herself on the bed. "Thank you for waiting. I love you so much." The tears fell again, but she barely knew.

In the muted light, the old woman's face looked like skin and bone. A mere shadow of the formidable woman she'd once been. Amber reached for her hand, shocked by the cold papery feel of her skin, and held it close. She leaned forward and pressed her lips to the old woman's forehead. She stroked her hair, filled with such love, such overwhelming gratitude. Her grammy's eyes opened a fraction and her blue, blue gaze was there, capturing hers, a small tear forming when she realised who it was. A sigh passed her lips, and she gave Amber's hand the faintest squeeze.

"Oh, Grammy, I love you so much." She wept, unable to hold back the emotion, the selfish desire to hold onto her forever. "I'll miss you so much, but it's okay. You've got this. You're the bravest woman I know."

Amber lay beside her and drew her close. Holding her. Holding on to her. Don't go, she wanted to yell. Don't leave me. So selfish, when her grammy was tired after a long life.

She sensed her grammy soften and relax against her, and Amber couldn't stop the sob or the tears. "It's okay, Grammy. I know you have to go. God has grand plans for you." She heard the soft sigh, her grammy's last breath. The silence. The stillness that followed. "I'll miss you. You'll always be here, with me, in my heart. Always." Don't go, she cried inside. Please don't go.

Amber held her grammy close, tears pouring in a silent torrent, the pain so fierce she could scarcely breathe. She heard the door open. Felt a hand on her shoulder. The warmth, the love seeping in.

"You were the light of her life, love." Her father's voice.

A fresh wave of tears fell, and she couldn't speak, not through the grief that lacerated her throat. Her grammy was gone, and it felt like a part of Amber's soul had been torn away. She'd never felt so alone. Life would be monochrome without the rich colour of her grammy's presence. Grammy had made her feel special and loved. In reality, she cried for her own loss. Amber should have been happy that the older woman's passing had been quiet, her last breath the softest of sighs. A letting go. An acceptance of God's will.

She thought of her grammy's love and the special moments they'd shared, and the memories she'd hold close long after her grammy was buried in the quiet cemetery on the hill.

"Come, my love." Her father's voice was a soft whisper in her ear. "Your mum made you some tea." He helped her to her feet.

Her grammy looked peaceful in death, her face serene. "I'll miss her," Amber choked, tears welling again. "So much."

"Yes." Tears shone in his eyes. He took her into his arms and held her close. "Me, too." They stood together for a long moment, taking solace in each other. Thinking of the past. Holding close their memories of happier times until Amber stepped back. She fished for tissues and blew the congestion from her nose. Her father brushed the tears from Amber's face and looked into her eyes as if seeking reassurance that she was okay.

"Shall we find Mum and Nate, darling?"

"Yes." She felt drained of emotion, weak and numb as they made their way to the kitchen. Amber lowered herself into a chair at the linoleum table, and Nate poured her a hot tea from a pot nestled in a hand-crocheted cosy. She thanked him and sipped, the hot liquid a welcome blessing. Her mother smothered a scone, still warm from the oven, with jam and cream, and pushed it towards her.

"Grammy passed away…" Amber's voice was barely a whisper and the sweet food barely registered as she went through the motions of eating and drinking, her body eerily disengaged from her aching heart.

Her mum and dad spoke in quiet tones. She felt disoriented and bruised, like she'd been hit by a truck. Nathan reached for her hand and held it, his warmth seeping through the chill.

She allowed herself to be bustled into her bed and tucked in like a small child. She drew the bedding close and drifted off as her mother showed Nate to the guest room. She didn't expect to sleep, but sleep came and with it a blissful forgetting until the moment she woke and the truth of it hit her again, leaving her sick to the stomach. She dressed and staggered into the country-style kitchen, and Nate was there, ready to take her in his arms. She allowed him to hold her, to warm her, to give her strength, too overwhelmed to remember why she didn't trust him.

"Thank you," she mumbled into the soft cashmere of his top, his scent musky and good. "For bringing me here. For being here. I appreciate it."

"I'm glad I could help." He stroked a lock of hair back from her face. She felt foolishly comforted. Foolishly warmed.

"Let me get you some breakfast." Amber drew away to find some coffee pods for the new-age machine that rested on the worn linoleum counter, bought with her own money and gifted to her family the previous Christmas. There was a plate piled high with bacon and eggs, left warm on the hob. She busied herself with toast and was conscious of Nate's gaze like a warm caress on her back. She allowed herself the luxury of not fighting it.

"Your dad's gone out to milk the cows," he said, and she

nodded. The farm was her father's special place, and his cows were more like children than animals. He would want some time alone. She looked out of the kitchen window to the paddocks beyond. It would be a warm day and already the shadows had lengthened across the yard. The chooks were wandering about, kicking up the earth with their feet, fossicking in the grass for something to eat. Lilydale was beautiful. A small town nestled amongst glades of trees, with rolling hills and cows dotted around. She heard the sound of their deep lowing and something inside her stilled. Home. The quiet eased her soul even as she remembered that the quiet had driven her away. Both heaven and hell, like life itself.

Like her past with Nathan. She didn't often think of the heaven she'd found in his arms, not when the hell had etched a deeper tract. The cost had been so great. The agony so much, but the good had been so good while it lasted. Better than good. Exceptional. Blissful. She'd believed herself in love back then, and she'd loved him with her entire soul. She'd embraced the feeling, so full of naïve trust and longing. That heady high, the yearning, the thrill. He'd filled the empty spaces inside her. He'd given her joy.

But he hadn't loved her.

His love had been like fool's gold—glittery and bright—but not real, and no man since had convinced her that love was worth the risk. Love could be selfish. Love could be abused. Love could hurt, and she was not fool enough to fall for it again, knowing the price. Love could be taken away and when it was? She reached for a coffee pod and slipped it into the machine.

Her grammy's words echoed in her mind. *Love is a gift, Amber, whether it lasts a few weeks or a lifetime. To love is a blessing.*

I know. I know. She breathed the rich scent of the freshly brewed coffee. *It's okay. I'll be fine.* She should be happy her grammy was free, not sad for herself.

"Are you alright?" Nathan's voice was warm and husky. She turned and refocused on the here and now.

"Yes. And I can't thank you enough." She reached for two plates. "Are you happy with bacon and eggs on toast, or would you prefer homemade jam or honey?"

He moved closer and his voice resonated inside her like a perfect tone or the haunting sound of a violin. "Bacon and eggs sound great, but why don't you sit down and have your coffee while I get them sorted."

"That's okay." She met his gaze through eyes that felt puffy and raw. She pushed the cup towards him. "Coffee?"

"Thanks." He leaned back against the kitchen table in the middle of the space and looked beyond the window to the view she knew so well. She loved this kitchen and would always associate it with her mother's baking and cups of coffee and warm conversation. With love of another kind.

She cut thick slices from the loaf of bread her mother had made fresh that morning and decided against toasting them, instead slathering them with homemade butter. "Orange juice?"

"Yes, thank you."

There was something intimate about breakfasting together. It felt right and relaxed until she thought about it, and then anxiety shot into her veins. *It's okay. It's fine. It's just breakfast. There's no need to stress. He wants nothing more than friendship.* But what did she want from him? Nothing more than this. No games. No promises too easily broken. He was as gorgeous now as he'd been a decade earlier. There wasn't a woman alive who wouldn't be attracted to him. But she was older and wiser, and she knew there was a difference between physical attraction and love. She wouldn't again confuse the first for the latter.

"We'll need to say our goodbyes after we eat." His voice was gentle, his gaze quiet. "It's past seven."

"Yes, you're right." Airlie Beach and the show seemed so far away. She couldn't remember why it was important. She felt disoriented. She hadn't thought of Nate's individual date, not once, and she hadn't spoken with Cassie.

Cassie would come up with something. She would handle it. Amber didn't need to micro-manage every single moment of the footage. Cassie's ideas were good. She sipped her coffee and managed to swallow another mouthful of bread. A comfortable silence fell between them.

When they finished eating, Nathan got to his feet and collected their plates. "I'll put these in the dishwasher while you say your goodbyes." He scraped the debris into a small bucket for the hens. "I'll catch up with you when you're done."

He was considerate, she realised. Quietly supportive. And unobtrusive. Respectful. It was something she'd think about later, but for now, she walked along the crushed stone pathway towards the milking shed. She could hear the cows lowing as they took themselves back towards the paddock on the hill. They didn't need herding—they knew the morning routine well—and she found her father cleaning the machinery.

"We need to get back." She allowed him to pull her close.

"Safe travels, Am. We'll let you know the burial details, but I understand if you can't make it. You got here to say goodbye and that's what's important. I love you, sweetheart."

"I love you, too." Her desire to stay warred with her need to go.

"Your mother's seeing to the hens."

"Okay. I'll find her. Thanks." The scent of the cow manure was overwhelming but stirred memories that comforted and warmed her. It was quiet now with the machinery turned off, but she heard long-ago echoes of the cows munching on their feed and the throb of the machines that relieved their udders, distended and full. She trudged the short distance back to the yard and across to the hen house. Her mother had already collected the eggs and was busy in the vegetable garden clearing weeds and picking tomatoes.

"Bye, Mum," she called, willing herself to stay strong.

"Bye, love." Her mother peeled off her leather gloves and came over to give her a hug. "Thank you for coming. It meant so much."

"I love you, Mum."

"I love you, too, precious girl."

"We need to get back. Once filming starts it's like a rolling stone. We can't afford to slow down. We need to keep moving."

"We understand. You go. Your Nathan is a lovely young man."

"He's not my Nathan, Mum." She stiffened in her mother's embrace and pulled away.

"Why not? He seems to like you a lot."

Amber shifted her focus to the harsh caw of the crows that soared overhead, their wings black against the vast blue of the sky. Her eyes squinted in the sunlight, sensitive after her tears. It was going to be a warm day. "Because... it's complex." She stepped back to give her mum a weak smile.

"It always is." Her mother's gaze held hers, green and clear. "Safe travels, my darling."

"Thanks for breakfast and the scones and everything.

Thanks for looking after Nathan."

"That was my pleasure, love. Now go. I can see him waiting at the gate." She waved and Nathan came towards them.

"Thank you for having us, Rose. Please say my goodbyes to Joe." He ushered Amber towards the house. And beyond. Down the hill. Past open paddocks and homes, most made of weatherboard and dating back to the middle of the last century. Sunlight filtered across the road, through trees that sprouted new growth, the fresh green of the leaves creating a canopy. The air was fresh, and there was the sound of cows lowing, the caw of the crows, the screech of cockatoos.

They walked towards the helicopter, and when Nathan took Amber's hand and cradled it in his, she let him. Heat travelled up her arm, and her insides grabbed and knotted. The lion's share of her attention had been on the scenery around her, and she forced herself to refocus. She hadn't been home in a while. The air was scented with flowers. Old rose bushes grew in gardens that hadn't changed in decades. There was the sweet smell of jasmine, and old magnolia trees spread wide and vast, loaded with big, white velvety flowers. The store fronts were worn, with rickety verandas and faded signs. It was a small township where everyone knew everyone.

"The general store has your name on it." Nate's voice broke her reverie, and her gaze shifted to the worn lettering. Lilydale and Reed were synonymous. Their name was plastered across the facia of several landmarks including the service station and the antique shop. Her family had lived here for generations.

"Yes, but we don't own it anymore." They approached the football ground where the helicopter stood waiting. She turned and observed the cemetery high on the hill. The tombstones were littered with her family's name. Most Reeds stayed, but those who didn't came back to rest, even those who took on a different name. She shook the melancholy from her thoughts and allowed herself to be ushered into the small cabin. Her emotions were quiet, exhausted after the night before, numb she realised, when Nathan buckled her in.

"Thank you," she said like an automaton.

"You look done in." He studied her for a long moment, before turning his attention to the knobs and dials. "Why don't you sleep? I don't mind."

"I'm not sure I can." Her gaze was on the landscape around them. Lilydale would not be the same without Grammy. But Amber had changed, too. She was no longer the free spirit who ran around in bare feet, oblivious to the ants and snakes. She looked down at her tightly laced trainers. Time had a way of changing things.

Chapter Six

Amber stood in the darkness beyond the lights and observed Nathan as he poured champagne and chatted with Mia. He appeared relaxed and chivalrous, and the footage so far screamed loud and clear that he was an all-round nice guy. She couldn't have asked for a better bachelor, and with Cassie's astrology-based selection process, she couldn't have asked for a better bevy of women. But the satisfaction she should have felt was increasingly elusive. He wasn't the man she'd known. Could ten years really change a person? She didn't think so. Not at such a fundamental level. Not without some form of catastrophe. His parents had separated, and his father had left them for his affair-of-the-moment. She supposed that might do it, or perhaps this man had always been there, deep inside, and she'd intuited it from the beginning. Perhaps the persona he'd presented at school had been just that, a persona. Goodness knows she'd had to develop a thick skin, or she would have been devoured by the judgemental opinions of those around her. Perhaps popularity came at a cost.

What if one of these women really was the love of his life? Was it Emily or Rebecca? Mia or Catherine? The women who'd signed up for the series were admirable. Smart. Beautiful. No doubt popular at school, given their confidence. Dan had found love. Would Nathan find love, too? She wanted that for him. Didn't she? She wanted him to find happiness. He'd been so kind to her. Damn, her thoughts were all over the place. She needed a good night's sleep. The key ceremony unfolded without a hitch. Cory wove his magic, and it seemed Genevieve was the woman to be singled out and farewelled. No surprise there.

"Cut. It's a wrap," she called, and the cameras stopped rolling. The girls sighed as they sank onto the couches and relieved their feet of their high heels. Some drained their glasses, and others reached for some food. "Great job," she assured them all. "The footage is terrific."

It had been a long night, and she was exhausted and emotionally drained. She walked out onto the deck with Cassie, the sky tinged with pink, the sun nearly over the horizon.

"What ideas did you come up with for the individual date tomorrow?" Amber asked, yearning for the peace and quiet of her own space.

"Actually, I wondered if you'd like a stint on the other side of the camera? I've seen how Nate looks at you. How you look at him. Is there anything going on between you that I should know about?" Her eyebrows lifted, and her searching gaze seemed to bore into Amber's soul.

"We had a thing…" She waved her hand in the air, as if she could brush away the past as easily as a mosquito. "A hundred years ago. At school." It sounded so simple.

"You went out together?" Cassie's eyes bulged. "You didn't think I should know about that? Did you…" She waited a heartbeat, her eyebrows lifting. "Oh, my."

Amber's gaze settled on the rising sun. "It's history—painful and foolish history—but he was kind enough to fly me to Lilydale, so I can't hold the past against him any longer."

"You're a Sagittarian, aren't you?" Her eyes gleamed.

"Don't even think about it. Not for one moment." Amber's stomach clenched, along with her fists. "He will propose to one of these contestants—on screen—as promised. Keep your eye on the ball, Cass. That's why we're here. Am I clear?"

"Crystal."

Amber didn't like the crisp edge to her tone. "No machinations. No plotting. No scheming."

"None." Cassie's brow furrowed and her eyes narrowed. "Are you sure?"

"Yes." No, she wasn't. "Totally." Amber schooled her face. "I'm sure. Let's get him safely married to someone else."

Cassie's gaze held hers for a long moment before she continued. "Mia and I decided on a Catamaran for her date tomorrow, and I was able to wangle a beauty, a sixty-two-foot Seawind 1600, along with a crew to handle the sails. There's a luxury saloon, and the forecast is perfect weather-wise. We get to show it off, and they get to advertise their business. We'll run their rates and contact details at the end of the episode. Mia suggested we take a trip out to Chalkie's Beach to snorkel then head across to Whitehaven Beach on Whitsunday Island for a walk. Maybe dinner at the yacht club at Hamilton Island, and a night sail back. What do you think?"

"It sounds fabulous. And we could go via the wild aquarium and get some footage of the Great Barrier Reef. They have an underwater pod, and Nate and Mia could have a moment with champagne and strawberries on a picnic blanket surrounded by fish. What time do we need to head off?"

"About ten. No need to brief Nate. It can be a surprise for

him."

"Excellent." Amber said with a sigh. "I'm done in."

"You get some sleep. I'll let Nate know about our starting time in the morning. Oh, and there was some shenanigans on the main deck last night. There was a massive mess in the lounge this morning—empty bottles of vodka mixers and champagne. I woke to a raucous at about four in the morning. Some of the crew were partying with the girls in the pool and spa. I pulled the plug on it and sent them all back to their rooms. I reminded the girls of their contractual obligations and told them how disappointed I was. I told them they were lucky it was me who discovered them and not you, or they would have been sent home. Ditto for the staff who promised it wouldn't happen again."

"Really? Surely not all of the contestants were involved. I can't imagine Mia or Catherine joining in."

"I think Suzanne instigated it, but no one pointed the finger. You'll remember she's a bit on the wild side. Still, we got some great footage if you want to use it."

"I'll speak with her and put her on notice. If she wants to leave, that will make the next key ceremony easy for Nathan! Perhaps he would be interested to hear about it, too. You can tell him when you see him."

"Sure, and you're right. Mia and Catherine weren't involved."

Amber trudged up the stairs to her room. She didn't see Niko and assumed Nathan must have taken him for a run. They were anchored near the Port Airlie (Abell Point) Marina and would need tender boats to get to where the Catamaran would dock in the morning.

It had been a long day and a long night. She checked her watch. Past six. No wonder she felt shattered. She stepped onto the aft upper deck, and drew in long, deep breaths of the warm salty air. She gazed across the water; her attention captured by the sound of male laughter below.

The rays of the morning sun stretched across the main deck, and she could see Nathan and Niko having a fine time wrestling over a ball on a piece of rope. They ended up in a tangled mess, and Niko's love for his master was apparent even from this height as he licked at him, and Nathan playfully growled about it. He finally extricated himself and threw the ball. Niko lunged after it, catching the ball before it landed, his ecstatic bark sounding across the still morning air. Amber watched, unable to drag her eyes from the sheer joy and exhilaration of their play.

Nathan had to be tired after their travels, and a very full afternoon out on the bay with the water toys from the beach club below—kayaks, paddle-boards, jet skis, and a giant banana ride pulled behind one of the tenders—then the cocktail party and the key ceremony, yet he'd still managed to prioritise some time with Niko. She couldn't help the stirring in her heart, and she chided herself for her foolish and wayward thoughts. He was warm-hearted and kind, and considerate and sexy, and so far out of her reach as to be from another planet.

If she wanted the show to succeed, she needed him to fall in love with one of the contestants. If she wanted ratings success, if she wanted her show to exceed the one that Jason stole from her and prove that *she* was the better producer, she couldn't fraternise with her lead man.

Besides, Nathan had nearly destroyed her once before, and she'd be past stupid to give him another opportunity to hurt her. She finally had her life together. No matter how grateful she was, she needed to remember what was important. With a heavy sigh, she turned towards her room and closed the door behind her, muffling the hoots and squeals coming from below.

She drew the curtains closed and began to undress before turning to the marble ensuite to ready herself for bed. *Goodnight, Grammy, wherever you are. I miss you. I love you.* She wiped the tears that welled in her eyes and reminded herself that her grammy was free. Free from the burdens of old age. Free from fear and vulnerability. She peered at her puffy eyes in the mirror, red-rimmed and wet. *Pull yourself together. You're fine. You've got this.* The show would be the best she'd ever produced, and Nathan would be a celebrity. Her mind turned to his product placement and his reasons for wanting it. Damn. Why did he have to be so nice?

Nice and Neanderthal Nathan in the same sentence?

Yes, nice, she thought, and sank into blessed oblivion.

"Okay," Nathan said. Cassie had filled him in on the basics about his individual date with Mia, but he had no clue what was ahead, and he found it quite disconcerting. He now had a better understanding of what it was like for the girls whenever they joined him. He knew exactly what was to come and had time to prepare himself, but they didn't.

They reached the beach club where the tender waited and Mia stood by the roped barrier, her gaze on the crystal-clear turquoise of the sea. The day was warm, with a gentle breeze that stirred the surface of the water. She wore a flowing white dress that reached almost to her ankles, strappy sandals, and a string of silk daisies around her head. Her blonde hair hung loose in a silken torrent down her back. She looked like a sea-goddess and his body reacted like he'd been struck.

"Hi," she said, her smile wide, her teeth white. He grinned

back and reached for her hand, drawing her towards him. The camera crew filmed from a discrete distance and there—at the front of the tender—was Amber. In work mode. Khaki shorts, a floaty white shirt, her hair pulled back in a ponytail, and aviator sunglasses. There was no outward sign of her personal loss, but behind the dark lenses her eyes would tell a different story.

He settled himself beside Mia at the back of the vessel, his arm draped around the seat behind her. "Where are we off to?"

"Ah, that's my surprise. We have a beautiful day for it." She grinned, her chocolate eyes bright, and he had to agree. The sun was shining, the sky was a cloudless blue, and the sea was like a beautiful aquamarine crystal.

There were cameras pointed at them from various angles, and they were well-wired so that every word that passed between them could be heard. He'd never get used to the constant scrutiny. It was an awkward way to start a date.

Amber was quiet in his ear—eerily so—and when he sought her out, her gaze was on the horizon.

The trip to the marina was a quick one, and he grinned when he saw the Catamaran. She was a beauty. The tender pulled up behind it, and they climbed aboard.

With the motor near-silent beneath them, the huge vessel moved out of its berth and towards the open water. They sat on deck and stretched out on leather seats, a low table with a bucket of champagne between them. It was Amber's voice in his ear, suggesting he open it and pour Mia a glass. At ten in the morning? He complied, while Mia shed some layers and settled across from him in a white bikini, her hair pulled back by the breeze like the proverbial figurehead at the bow of a ship. With the sweeping cry of gulls overhead, and the splash of the water as the hulls cut through the slight chop of the waves, his attention should have been on Mia rather than Amber, and he fought to redirect his focus.

Mia was slender but not reed-thin, and she had curves where a woman should. She was smoking in a bikini, and he'd rarely felt this at ease with a woman. She wasn't trying to impress him: she was just enjoying the moment.

"You're a yoga instructor?" he asked.

"Yes, but only part time. I work as a radiographer at the Royal Women's in Melbourne."

"You do ultrasounds for women who are pregnant?"

"Yes, amongst other things. It's so special to show a couple the beat of their baby's heart for the first time, and I get to reassure them that their child is developing the way it should. That part never grows old. I love my job." She sipped her champagne.

"It must be difficult if the news isn't good."

"Yes, very. It's so sad if a baby's heart isn't beating, or if there's some kind of problem, but knowledge is power, and the scan gives couples the information they need to make an informed decision."

"Your work is important then. It must feel good to contribute in such a way." He took a sip of his own drink, the feel of the cameras like grit in his eye.

"Yes," she agreed, "but I love my yoga too, and it keeps me fit."

"You look incredible." He kicked off his casual loafers, leaned back and adjusted his sunglasses. Mia's legs were golden brown and beautifully smooth with dark polish on her toenails, her skin luminous and healthy.

But it was Amber's breath in his ear, as choppy as the

waves, that drew his attention. She was struggling, and his thoughts veered from the perfect woman beside him to the woman who held his heart. She sat with her legs over the side of the boat, her arms on the metal railing, her attention outward. Cassie, bless her, stepped in seamlessly to direct the proceedings. He'd created an unbearable rod for his back. He wanted—needed—this show to be a success. He owed Amber that, yet to be a success, he had to find love with another woman.

Mia was lovely and interesting, and he fought to give her the attention she deserved. Why was he thinking of Amber at all? Because she was hurting. Because she was grieving. Because he cared. Mia watched him over the rim of her glass.

"Are you okay?"

"I'm more than okay. This is my idea of heaven." He lifted his glass and she raised hers. "To an amazing date." The breeze picked up and with the sails unfurled and full, they sped fast across the open water.

"It's exhilarating, isn't it?" She tipped her head back and basked in the sunshine. They were silent for a while, enjoying the moment, the rush of speed, the cool spray of the water. "I'd like to use my key to the stateroom sometime if it's not an imposition. Why did you choose to give it to me?"

"I felt a connection between us. I still do."

"Yes." Her gaze studied him before veering away.

"And I think you're one of the few girls who are here for the right reason."

"Yes, I'd say there are quite a few girls who hope to pick up a modelling or television gig or become a celebrity." She took a sip of her drink. "I'm looking for love and friendship. A companion and someone to build a life with. I want children."

"How many?" It was like someone had reached into his chest and grabbed his heart. He hadn't thought about children. He needed a wife. Not a family. But of course, Mia would want a family, and she deserved one. She'd make a beautiful mother.

"Four," she answered. "I was an only child, and I was envious of those who had brothers and sisters."

"I'm the oldest of two," he told her. "I have a sister, Isabella. She's had some health issues since my parents separated about seven years ago. She was younger than me at the time and more traumatised."

"How old is she now?" Mia appeared genuinely interested.

"Twenty."

"What kind of health issues?"

His thoughts spun for a moment before he answered. Should he speak of it publicly? It would help others to be more aware of the dangers and to look out for the signs, and he was sure Bella would want him to. He'd been too slow to appreciate the danger, too late to realise what Bella was dealing with. He'd blamed his father, when in truth, it was his own fault. *He* should have paid more attention. "She developed anorexia. She thought she was fat when in truth she was skin and bone. She over-exercised and barely ate." He paused, and Mia leaned across to take his hand in the comfort of hers.

"She nearly died many times. It's been a huge battle. My mother and I feared we would lose her."

"What about your father?" Mia asked.

"He moved on with his new partner who is not much older than I am. She believed Bella was trying to steal my father's attention away from her, and she had little sympathy. I think Bella needed to feel she had control over something, but it became an illness."

Perhaps his father would see the show and understand what he'd missed. Or not. Nate no longer cared whether his father lived or died, but he sure as hell cared whether his stepmother inherited everything or not. His grandfather would turn in his grave if he knew how foolish Nate's father had been, or maybe he'd anticipated it, and that was why he'd put the marriage clause into Nate's inheritance—to force him to grow up before he took over the reins. It had been a risky move, given the child-man Nate's father was, and the very good chance the family fortune would be whittled away before Nate took over.

But if Nate's grandfather had been less busy earning money and more busy parenting his only child, Nate's father might have been less spoiled and indulged, and more capable of becoming a responsible adult. It seemed like bad-father genes ran in his family. And that was why Nate didn't want children, and why he'd referenced it in the fine print of his prenup. But then it struck him, as sharp as the slap of the water against the twin hulls of the Catamaran, it wasn't fair to these women if being a mother was important to them. Mia wanted love and children, and she was a beautiful woman. She deserved to have her four children, but the thought made his skin crawl.

Men in his family didn't deserve to procreate.

"That must have been hard." Mia's compassion wrapped around him like a warm hug.

"It was." He said it simply before redirecting the conversation to less sensitive topics.

It was easy to get caught up in the romance—the decadent surroundings, the brush of the breeze, the generous and caring woman at his side—Amber was good. He'd let down his guard as she'd probably hoped he would.

He forced a smile onto his face. Mia wanted to please him.

She'd thought this would be fun. For her sake, he had to push himself out of the darkness of his mind, and into the brightness of the day. And what a day it was.

When they stopped at a pontoon seemingly in the middle of nowhere, he realised it was an underwater observatory, a wild aquarium. He fought a wave of nausea as he stepped onto the pontoon and down into a glass walled pod. He was surrounded by sea creatures, and while Mia ooh'ed and ah'ed he fought the rush of his pulse. It took him straight back to the past and anxiety rippled under his skin lifting his hair follicles.

"Are you okay?" Mia's expression was one of bafflement. "I thought it would be amazing to be surrounded by beautiful fish. It's so tranquil and peaceful down here."

She looked at him, and with the simple ring of flowers around her head, she was a stunning woman. He should be grateful for the opportunity to spend time with her, but then out of the corner of his eye, he saw a shark and its distinctive movement as it came towards the glass. Sweat broke out on his brow, and his stomach kicked and rolled as he fought the instinct to flee. Dizziness left him light-headed and faint.

"What's wrong?" It was Amber's voice in his ear. "Cut," she called and rushed over to check on him. "What is it?" She drew him away from the cameras and the microphones and gave him a sip of cold water. "You look terrible. Are you okay?"

"I don't like sharks." The words didn't come close to saying what he needed to say, but the thought of a shark, a big one, not a metre away was enough to make his head pound and panic rise in his throat. He had to focus. On his breath. Like he'd been taught. "I'll be fine. I just need a moment to get myself together."

"It's behind the glass," she assured him. "And you don't have to swim out there if you'd rather not."

"Swim?" His voice reached soprano pitch.

"There's scuba gear on the boat, and Mia planned to take you diving. It's rare to see a shark. The footage should be amazing—the coral and the fish in stunning colours that you don't often see. But if you'd rather not, we can arrange for someone else to swim with her. Films use stunt people all the time, so you don't need to feel pressured."

Amber's green gaze held his and his feelings for her sucker-punched his traumatised gut. He wanted to reach out and take her face in his hands. He wanted to soothe the pain he could see in the shadowy depths of her eyes. She was hurting, and here she was worried about him.

"You're right. The footage would be amazing. Can someone else come into the water with us and keep the damn sharks away?"

"Yes," she promised. "I'll organise it. Are you sure? It sounds like you have a phobia. You don't have to do it. Not for me. Not for Mia. Not for the show. There's no pressure for you to do anything you'd rather not do."

"I can do it." He took deep calming breaths. The chance of a shark attack inside a wild aquarium was unlikely. Tourists swam out there all the time, but this was open water. This wasn't an indoor aquarium where the sharks were used to people. These weren't hand-fed or domesticated. They hunted for their food. "I just need a moment to get used to the idea. I'll be fine. I'm good. Sorry for the drama." He considered her for a long moment. "How are you feeling?"

"I'm fine if I keep busy," she replied. "Thanks for asking."

"Good," he said with renewed strength. "Let's get back to it."

"Are you sure you're okay?"

"I will be." When the damn swim was over.

Mia stood near the glass watching the fish, a slightly confused look on her face when he re-joined her. "Sorry about that. I'm fine. I felt faint for a moment. I needed some water. We don't have to catch our lunch, do we?"

"No." She laughed. "But they're all safe with me. I'm a vegetarian."

"Let's do this." He clamped down on the panicky sensations that skittered around inside him. He turned and the area had been transformed into a romantic nook, with cushions and champagne. He settled into the set and focused on the fresh strawberries. They were huge and he picked one up and lifted it to Mia's mouth, the moment mesmerising. With his attention on the woman across from him, and not on the sea life circling around them, he felt stronger. Mia reached for a strawberry and returned the favour—the fruit was sweet and ripe and packed a punch. Delicious. He poured champagne and fought to relax. The cameras circled them; the crew dressed in black. He reached for Mia's hand, and they settled into conversation.

But the evil moment came all too quickly, and before he knew it, he was shimmying his way into a wetsuit, the neoprene against his skin making his pulse skyrocket. He helped Mia with her tank and swung one onto his own back. He lowered the mask over his eyes and fitted the mouthpiece with a silent prayer. He took Mia's hand and together, they dropped into the water. The feel of the water against his chest was enough to give him heart palpitations, and he had to speak firmly to himself. *Focus on Mia. Focus on her pleasure.*

Mia's eyes shone with joy when she saw the coral, and the fish that swam around it. The beautiful colours shimmered in the fractured light from the surface, and he squeezed Mia's hand.

Bubbles rose from their equipment and it was eerily quiet. He kept his gaze on Mia and the joy in her eyes. You can do this. Nearly there. Not much longer. He counted his breaths as he'd been taught. Focused on areas of his body in turn. Relaxed the muscles around his stomach. Relaxed his shoulders. Relaxed his arms.

Fish food appeared in the water around them, small morsels that slowly sank in the rays of the sun that penetrated from above. Fish swarmed towards them—purple, pink, orange, the colour of the rainbow—gobbling greedily at the treats, their eyes large and luminous, some fluid of movement, some darting and slick—and tension arced through his muscles.

Nate saw the shark in the periphery of his vision and a fist tightened around his throat. He took Mia in his arms, focusing his attention on the feel of her lithe body and pointed up. Entwined, they rose together and broke the surface of the water shortly after. He ripped the hose from his mouth and grabbed at the air with hungry lungs, his chest heaving.

He forced himself to wait while Mia pulled herself out. *It's okay. They're more interested in the food than in you.* But his heart was in his throat, and he couldn't breathe past it. Finally, he was on the ladder, and he heaved himself out of the water and collapsed on the deck of the boat. He gulped like a fish on dry land, unable to ease the tight band around his chest.

Amber's voice was in his ear. Soft and soothing. "You're okay, Nate. The shark was interested in the food. He was slow and lazy at best." Nate looked down against every instinct. The shark swam around below, the water so clear he could see its movement as it swam. The sight of it brought chills to his skin. Mia pulled herself up beside him and unpeeled her wetsuit. He tried to focus on the unbelievable sight of her golden, yoga-toned body in her white bikini, but he was too done in with the effort of controlling his breath. No doubt the cameras were honing in on Mia so he focused and pulled himself together.

It seemed snorkelling was on their agenda as well, but the shallows at Chalkie Beach were a whole different ball game to the reef. There, he could relax and enjoy the schools of fish that gathered around them, his hand encompassing Mia's. Their walk along Whitehaven Beach was an absolute treat—the coastline was one of the most pristine in the world and a national park bordered its shores. The sand was the purest white and the water was crystal clear. Mia was good company, but he yearned for some time with Amber. She walked ahead or behind, lost in her own thoughts, which was very unlike her. She usually orchestrated his romance from afar.

The sun was well into its downward arc by the time they stepped off the boat at Hamilton Island, and boarded a golf buggy to head to the yacht club for dinner. They sat at the roof-top bar sipping pre-dinner cocktails and watched the rosy glow of the sunset. Dinner was fine dining at its best, and it was dark by the time they reboarded the Catamaran and sailed back towards Airlie Beach. The moon was near-full, which they couldn't have orchestrated if they'd tried, and the glittery path of silver made for a perfect backdrop. Masses of stars, and a warm night. Nate had had a nice time—a really nice time—but as he huddled with Mia on the way back to Port Airlie, his thoughts were with Amber.

The night was crammed with another group date—with lays and a limbo pole and lots of laughter—and a key ceremony led by Cory, where Nathan trimmed another two girls from the pack. After a restless sleep, Nate rose early and took a tender to Airlie Beach with Niko.

He tossed a Frisbee and straightened the towel he'd looped around his neck. The morning was warm, and he wanted a swim—there were no stingers around at this time of year—which led his thoughts back to Mia and their surprise date. He didn't think he'd survive another, but it did give him a better sense of what it was like for the girls. Leaping out of planes, canyoning… they'd all soldiered on and enjoyed themselves, or pretended to enjoy themselves, for his sake. Well, he'd pay better attention in future and would assure them it wasn't necessary to take part on his account. Hell, he'd probably admire them more if they spoke up and were genuine about their fear instead of trying to impress him.

Still, he'd wanted to impress Mia, hadn't he? No, it was more that he hadn't wanted to let her down. She'd been so excited and had tried to please him. They'd had a lovely day except for the aquarium fiasco. Dinner had been outstanding, but he was glad when the evening was over, and he could give Mia the cabin key, and wrap it up. The key ceremony back on board had been easy, particularly after Cassie filled him in on the party that had taken place during their absence. Suzanne was at the top of his chopping list. So far, the culling had been clear-cut and easy. He wouldn't miss any of the women he'd sent home.

He sensed a storm in the air as the breeze whipped up, and he heard the distant rumbling of thunder. The night had been hot, and the air was thick and still. He and Niko frolicked like children, and he was surprised when he turned and Amber was there, standing on the sand, her feet bare and her smile warm.

Niko gallantly dashed over, Frisbee in his mouth. He dropped it at her feet, tore away, and tore back, crouching in front of her, his yelp of excited enthusiasm as good as a verbal request.

"Okay, okay," she said with a laugh and bent down to pick it up. She steered it along the water line, away from Nate who stood still, fearful any movement might frighten her away. Niko took off after it with a happy bark, and Amber moved towards him, wearing a short flowy dress.

"Hi." The word caught in his throat. She was beautiful. Ethereal in the rays of sunlight that broke through the churning cloud above. The breeze caught at her ponytail and pulled at her dress.

"Hi." Her attention shifted to the sky. "There's a storm brewing, and I couldn't resist the draw of it."

Lightning flashed over the sea, still some distance away and thunder growled.

"I wondered if you'd notice we were missing," Nate replied. It was a comfort, having her in the periphery of his senses, just out of his vision or just beyond his hearing, the silk of her sigh like a caress against his skin.

Niko barrelled towards them, skittery and excited. Nate reached for the toy and flung it good and far. Niko rushed to retrieve it. "Let's go for a walk. The beach is lovely here, and we'll soon be back out at sea.

"You're good with him." Amber fell into step beside him. "You make him feel special."

"He is," Nate replied.

"You have a few more group dates and individual dates before we get to the final four contestants, then we have the home visits."

"When's the funeral?"

"Not until after we wrap up in Broome, so I'll head there afterwards. Hopefully, the timing will work."

"I think it's important for you to go." He'd make sure of it. They walked in silence and Niko rushed ahead, checking in on them every few minutes. Nate's feet sank into the cool, damp sand and he stood close to Amber, his eyes on Niko who frolicked in the water.

He yearned to take her in his arms and hold her, knowing how much she needed it, but he daren't risk the precarious peace between them.

Niko chose that moment to drag himself out of the water and shake drops all over them. Amber cried out with laughter and Nate was taken with the sudden urge to pick her up and run them both into the water. Hell, why not. He had the element of surprise and Amber screamed when she realised what he intended. Niko joined in the fray and yelped happily as he leapt around them. Nate fell over his feet and dumped Amber unceremoniously into the cool depths. She came up gasping for breath, her laughter filling him with the urge to laugh, too. He reached for her and drew her close, their laughter stalling as their breaths merged and the magic he always felt when his lips came close to hers shimmered around him, slowing the spin of the world on its axis, slowing time and narrowing space until there was only Amber.

"I want to kiss you," he said, his voice husky, his mouth a tantalising nanometre from hers.

Her gaze clung to his, her body athletic and trim against him. Despite the cold of the water, he was rock hard and there was no doubting his sexual interest. Thunder echoed around them and for a moment the sky lit up, the flash capturing the intensity of Amber's gaze. On him. On his lips. She wanted him, and knowing it changed everything. She wanted him as much as he wanted her. Despite her anger and disappointment, her grief, and her determination to make her show a success. The elation near lifted him out of the water.

The first few drops of rain were enormous, like huge, swollen tear drops reminding him of her vulnerability and grief. This wasn't the time to push her towards something he shouldn't want, and with reluctance he stepped back although he couldn't fight the urge to catch her hand. He held it in his, acknowledging the perfect fit, the slender form of it as he drew her from the waves, water cascading down her body. He almost stopped, he almost followed the cry in his blood to take what he wanted and to hell with the consequences. But this was Amber, and she deserved better than that.

He reached for the towel he'd left on the sand and wrapped it around her shoulders. The raindrops were heavier now, and the gap between the growl of the thunder and the flash of the lightning was shorter. They needed to get back to the boat. He called to Niko, and his feet fought for traction in the shifting sand.

"You wanted to kiss me."

Her words paralysed him, and time froze into an explosive moment, ripe with possibility. Temptation wove around him. This is Amber, he lectured himself. Amber. He would not ruin her life twice.

"I did." His body felt like he'd been struck by lightning. Burnt out and hollowed. He had no right to kiss her. He had no right to want her.

"Why didn't you?" Her voice was a mere thread of its normal

strength.

"Because kissing you is complicated."

"It is." She sighed and shifted her gaze towards the horizon. "You're right, of course." There was resignation in her voice, and he wanted to kiss her anyway, but that wouldn't be fair. He wanted to prove to her that he'd changed. He wanted to treat her with the respect she deserved, and besides, he wasn't willing to risk the connection they already shared. It was damned complicated, and he hadn't figured it out yet. He wanted her and not just for a surreptitious kiss that would leave her feeling humiliated afterwards.

Then what the hell did he want? Damn it. He didn't know. He wanted her show to be a success. He wanted that much for her, but to find love with one of the contestants meant giving her up, and now that he'd found her again... he didn't want to give her up. Best they go back, he thought, where he could leave her focused on business and walk away.

"I shouldn't have interrupted your time with Niko."

"I'm glad you did." And he was, but walking was far from comfortable, and if she had any idea what she did to him, she'd run from him like she should have done when she was a teenager.

"About Bella," she said, and he stilled in his tracks. Of course, Amber had overheard his conversation with Mia. In truth, he'd been speaking to her. He'd wanted her to know.

"I'm really sorry she was unwell, and you had to deal with that on your own." She paused. "It must have been so hard for you. Back then. I understand now why it was so important for you to market your powders and potions. It's about more than money. It's about giving Bella and the others a sense of autonomy and achievement. That clinic you spoke of? They helped her, didn't they? You want to help Bella pay it forward. I get it now."

"Yes," he said simply. "I could have given them the money, but that wouldn't have helped Bella, and it wouldn't have helped any of the kids find what's important. Self-respect. Autonomy. Bella stepped up, and she runs the business. She mentors the others. This clinic saves lives. It saved her life."

They walked together towards the tender, hand in hand, the air around them thick with the approaching storm. He sensed her softening and struggled against it. He didn't want or need her understanding. He didn't want or need the feelings she roused in him. He wasn't worthy of her. Hell. The woman tied him in knots.

He dropped her hand when they reached the tender, pulled up on the beach, and she turned. Her drenched hair framed her heart-shaped face and spilled over the smooth curve of her shoulder. Her sea-green eyes held his and her lips, the colour of a ripe pomegranate, called to him with hazardous temptation.

"I wanted to kiss you, too." A frown marred the smoothness of her forehead.

"I know." He was enchanted by the honest confusion in her eyes.

Niko chose that moment to leap against them, his tongue laving Amber's face and the spell was broken. She smiled at them both and spun away to climb into the small boat. He joined her and Niko settled with his head on her lap. The wind churned the protected water of the bay into white caps.

Niko, mate, your timing was impeccable. I was about to do something that would have changed everything. Who was he kidding? Everything had changed, whether he'd followed

through with the kiss or not. He wanted her.
And she wanted him back.

Chapter Seven

Amber sat on the top rail of the corral in dusty jeans and a faded singlet top. The trip out to Dimbulah in the Atherton Tablelands had taken not quite two hours from Cairns, and the temperature remained pleasantly warm. The sun was low in the sky now, the shadows across the farmyard elongated, and the insects were loud in the growing dusk. The group date at the working farm had turned out to be a lot of fun, and she'd managed to distract herself from the unpleasant truth of her wanton wishes where Nathan was concerned by staying busy. They'd taken a trail ride, and the wildlife had been outstanding with kangaroos, rock wallabies, and wedge-tailed eagles. Some of the girls were very comfortable on a horse, and they'd cantered ahead, while the rest of them had moseyed along at a slower pace.

Nathan was wrestling a sheep into position for whoever's turn it was to attempt shearing. There were those who embraced the opportunity, and those who looked devastated at the risk of breaking a fingernail. They'd milked a cow, herded pigs, collected eggs, and mucked out a stable. Grooming the old Clydesdale had sorted the animal lovers from the princesses, and Amber had chuckled aloud when a sheep dog had bustled into the shot and a couple of the girls had acted like he was a pit bull. No doubt they'd hate Niko.

"Amber, the band's arrived." Cassie spoke breathlessly. "And John asked if you could meet with him about the set-up for the dance."

"Sure. Thanks." Amber swung her legs back to the ground. "Could you take over here?" She handed Cassie the mic and rushed over to where Mal, the stage manager, stood with a small crowd of muso's and her piece de resistance, Keith Urban.

"It's lovely to meet you all. Thanks so much for coming." She couldn't keep the excited schoolgirl pitch from her voice. She shook Keith's hand, and every hair follicle on her body lifted and fell in a Mexican wave. He was even more gorgeous in person than on screen. It had been quite the coup, catching him during a break in his touring schedule, and she'd pulled strings, a whole quartet of them to have him here for the evening.

She loved country music and these guys were the real deal. She'd promised plenty of coverage for their new album and with millions of viewers all over the country, it was a win-win for all of them. She led them into the barn and organised a round of cold beers.

The spit-roast dinner was well underway, and the smell of the barbecuing meat was amazing, although half the girls were vegetarian, and she'd catered for them as well. There would be line dancing in cowboy boots and tight jeans. Good television, she assured herself. Colourful and musical, and who didn't love an evening under the stars?

The side of the barn would be open to the night and there would be a fire in a pit outside for toasting marshmallows, with bales of hay to sit on. Plenty of cosy corners for Nathan to draw his chosen woman in for a kiss... and that's when her stomach clenched like a fist ready for a bar fight, or perhaps it was the sight of Jason strolling across her set as cool as an ocean breeze. Shouldn't he be off filming in some glamorous location?

"What are you doing here?" You show-stealing low-life. Temper roared in her ears.

"Just thought I'd drop by since I was in Cairns, and I heard through the grapevine that you were, too." He grinned. "I thought you'd be interested to hear how well *The Amazing Race* is doing."

"I'm sure it's doing brilliantly, given it was *my* idea."

"There's no need for that, Amber," he chastised. "Tomayto. Tomarto. What's good for the network is good for both of us."

"There is no *us*, Jason." The words twisted from her mouth. "You got what you wanted, and I've moved on."

"Come on, Amber," he soothed. "It's not like you didn't have a swathe of other ideas. How was I to know you planned to present that one to Ron?"

Why was she even having this conversation? He didn't deserve the time of day. He was in her way, under her feet, interfering with her schedule. "I'm busy, Jason. And we're done here, so I'd appreciate it if you'd..." Slide back into the stinking hole from which you came. "Leave." She used a prim, no nonsense tone and eyed her security team. How the hell had he gotten past them in the first place?

"We're far from done, Am." He moved closer and encircled her with his arm. "Come on, babe. I've missed you."

"Back off, Berringer."

"We had something good going. Don't be like that. You know you want me."

"You're wrong." She pulled away. "You're a lying, cheating, show-stealing bastard. Now, get off my set." How had she ever

111

found him attractive? The thought of his hands on her was enough to make her want to slide out of her own skin. "Now if you don't mind, I'm working."

"What time will you be done? I could take you out for a late-night drink, and you can tell me all about your new show. It's going to air next week, isn't it?"

"Jason, I don't want to call security, but you've left me no choice."

"I miss you, babe. I love you." His rich caramel gaze held hers, and his smooth, honey tone washed over her. In the past, she would have softened, but now all she felt was chilled. "We had something special between us. Something real. I'm sorry it took me so long to realise."

"I'm sorry, too." Shivers crawled over her skin. "Let me walk you out." How had she ever fallen for his smarmy self-serving tripe? He was here to snoop, and she didn't trust him. Not for one moment. No doubt he'd love to see her fall on her face, and she had no intention of giving him that pleasure.

"You have hay in your hair." He pulled the offending piece away. "A barn dance, babe? Really? You don't think that's a bit kitsch?"

"Don't touch me." She dug the heels of her Blundies deep into the dry earth as she escorted him towards the security guards at the gate. How the hell had he wormed his way past them in the first place?

"Okay, I know how it is when you're absorbed in your work. I'll wait until you're done, then we can talk. We need to talk," he insisted.

"I have nothing to say to you except good-bye."

"Oh, come on, babe, you know you don't mean that."

"Oh, I mean it alright. Happy travels." She scowled at the

security staff. "No one comes in here without my okay, am I clear? Especially not him."

"Sorry, Amber." The man was middle aged and stocky. He gave her an apologetic smile. "He had a security pass and said you were close friends."

"Well, we're not." She gritted her teeth. "Next time, check with me first."

"Absolutely. Yes, ma'am."

Jason climbed into a late model Mercedes sports car and revved the engine. His wheels spun in the gravel and he left without a backward glance. No doubt he'd made a killing from his show—*her* show—which had been a great success. Sour grapes, she thought, and trekked back the way she'd come. The sun had dropped behind the horizon, and she needed to keep things moving. She heard stifled laughter and arrived on set in time to see Nathan and Nina disappear around the corner of the barn with beers in their hands. Where were the cameras?

She gesticulated to Cassie who dashed over. "Don't worry, we've got it covered. She pointed upwards, and Amber caught sight of a camera guy on a small balcony with a long-range lens.

"Good," she said with a sigh.

"Was that Jason Berringer you were talking to? He has a nerve after what he did."

"An ego more like." Amber tightened the band around her ponytail. "Are the girls ready?"

"Almost. Makeup is done. The music is brilliant. I can't believe you got Keith and his band." Cassie's face was alight with excitement. "We're going to have us an outback party."

"We sure are." Amber needed this show to be brilliant. Better than brilliant. She needed to lift the bar to the stratosphere.

And to do that, she needed these girls to fall head over their spurred heels in love with Nathan. She gave a thumbs-up to Mal, the staging manager, and grinned at Keith. The music was fine, and the evening was clear. The first smattering of stars shone overhead, bright in the deep blue of the twilight. The fire crackled in the pit, and she grabbed herself a cold drink, along with a plate of food. Life was good, and there was no way Jason Berringer was going to upset that.

Mal shuffled the girls into position with Nathan centre front. Okay, Amber thought. The colours were perfect, the lighting warm, and the joyful jig that sprang from the electric violin was pure provocation. Even she yearned to kick up her heels and laugh with the rest of them.

The dance teacher had them looking professional and no one found the steps too challenging. Indeed, Sienna, who was a professional dancer, shone like the sun, and men the country over would melt into their TV snacks. Her kicks were high, and her smile was enough to make every man out there swoon. Not to mention the rest of the ladies. They were easy on the eye. Very easy on the eye. And Nathan had an appeal of his own.

Nathan's focus was on Sienna—she couldn't blame him—and Amber let out a sigh.

"Are you okay?" Nate spoke in her ear. How had she forgotten the mic was on? She gave him a thumbs-up and an encouraging smile even as the claws of jealousy sank into her flesh.

"It's going well. Keep it up." The scene was done, and Amber stood with Nathan, a drink in her hand. "You make an irresistible cowboy."

"I sure hope so. Are you up for a tumble in the hay?"

"Ha, ha. Keep your focus on the main game, cowboy." She took a swig of her cold beer.

"I find it wandering." His gaze skimmed hers.

She couldn't help the beam of pleasure that wormed its way in. "Jason was here earlier to gloat, and it reminded me why this show has to be better than brilliant. We've got some great footage, but we need to keep working. Make sure you sit with the girls around the fire and toast some marshmallows. Here." She handed him a bowl and some very long handled forks. Keith kindly chose that moment to go with something more soulful, and she found herself swept up in the haunting music. "Oh, that's perfect." Keith Urban was a legend.

"No, you are." Nathan's voice was so quiet, she wasn't sure she'd heard him correctly.

"Move it, cowboy." She grinned. "The timing's right for you to get up close and personal with some of the girls."

"You're the boss."

Nathan settled onto a hay bale next to Sienna, his hand resting on the slim length of her thigh. And Amber suffered a very bad case of thigh envy.

"It's going well." Cassie stepped up beside her, just outside the circle of light.

Amber nodded, her gaze fixed on the love action in front of her. She wanted the show to succeed—she needed it to succeed—but she *wanted* and that was the irony of it. She wasn't the only one who wanted, and the boom operator skilfully captured the jealous whispers from a couple of the other girls. If looks could kill, Sienna would be hung, drawn, and quartered. After tonight, she'd be a target for the others who'd recognise the danger she posed. Flexible. Gorgeous. A dancer's body. Oh, yes, she was a threat. A lethal one.

The claws inside her dug deeper, and she nearly bent with the intensity of it.

"If he has trouble choosing between them, I'm happy to throw my hat in the ring," Cassie whispered. "He's gorgeous, Amber. Kind and considerate. We have the perfect bachelor on our hands—even better than Dan. More aloof. In a Darcy kind of way. Smouldering and sexy and fabulous… Did you hear Dan's marrying Christina?"

Amber shook her head. "He sure fell hard."

"Nate asked for a day off to be part of their wedding party. I hope you don't mind." She grinned. "How cool is it that he owns a helicopter and can pilot it himself?"

"Get your tongue off the ground. You're drooling all over me."

"How did the edits go?" Cassie asked unrepentantly.

"You can add incredibly photogenic to his list of positive attributes." Amber's gaze shifted to the moon, which hung low and full beyond the branches of the gum trees. "Check the moon out. It's perfect. Eerily large and yellow." The scene was beyond extraordinary and beyond perfect.

"I'll be back." Amber dashed off, careful not to trip over the cables that ran here and there and spoke to the director of photography who nodded and bustled about. She rubbed her hands with glee. There was the beauty of the night sky, the beauty of the flames, the beauty of the women who sat around the fire on bales of hay… and the lust, the jealousy, the bountiful extremes of human nature on display in that small circle of light.

"You're a genius." The voice came from behind her. She spun

on her heels to find Jason lounging against a fence post, a piece of grass in his mouth.

"What are you doing here?" Her tone was waspish, and she raked the darkness for her men in black.

"Come on, babe. I had a lovely chat with Nina—such a delightfully clumsy woman and very informative—and now I'd really like to have a chat with you. It's important."

He reeked of alcohol and his breath was stale. "Let me think." Amber feigned concentration. "Nope. Still not interested, but thanks anyway. Now get off my set."

"You're cute when you're mad." His words were slurred.

"No, I'm angry when I'm mad and if you don't leave, I'll call the network and complain to Ron. Don't you have a stolen show to produce? Last I heard, you were in Paris or was that London or Rome?"

"The perks were inspired. That was very smart of you."

His tone was a sneer and for the first time, Amber felt unsafe. "I asked you to leave."

"Do you need a helping hand?" Nate appeared beside her, and his voice was like plush velvet, deep and sensual as it resonated through her body. His timing was perfect.

"Nathan, this is Jason." An unpleasant blast from the past. "Thank you, but he was just leaving." For the second time today.

"Well, let me see you to your vehicle." Nate's smile wasn't friendly. "We're real busy here, and I didn't like your tone of voice."

The mic, of course. She'd forgotten about it.

"I'm not here to cause trouble." Jason's words ran together. "I just thought Amber might like a lift after she was done here, that's all."

"Well, it sounds like that's a no, and I'm pretty sure Amber asked you to leave."

Amber watched as Nathan herded Jason towards the security staff.

"What are you doing back here, mate?" one said. "Amber asked you to leave hours ago."

This was the second time Amber had asked the fellow to leave? "I believe you're trespassing. Amber's made it very clear you're not welcome here."

"You're very protective for a guy who's spoilt for choice." Jason eyed him suspiciously. "Don't tell me you've fallen for Amber's infinite charms." He guffawed. "Oh, that's a riot. Does she know?"

Nate gave him a push towards the security staff, and they took it from there. Damn. Was he that transparent?

"Ignore him, Nate. He makes self-serving an art form." Amber's voice stirred the remnants of his anger.

"You went out with him?"

"He can be charming when he tries," she answered. "He hides his spots well, but I've seen the real man, and it's not pretty."

"He's a polished act." Nate watched him get into his sports car. "Many a woman would fall for that. And many a man would fall for the amazing women you hand-selected for the show. My job is getting tougher. I'm not sure who to send home tonight."

"Oh, I'm glad to hear that."

She looked gorgeous with her hair pulled back, a black shirt over her singlet top, and her jeans, snug on her hips. She did country chick well, and it turned out he liked country. He liked the music. The open fire. The dancing. She'd created a masterpiece.

"Are you plotting a quiet moment with an irresistible woman behind a bale of hay by any chance?" She grinned, but her tone was wry.

"Just me—her—and how many millions of people?"

"I'll get back to you after next week's premiere."

"Are you nervous about it, Am?"

"I wouldn't be human if I wasn't, and Jason's snooping tonight has reminded me why it's so important to succeed. I want the show to do well. I need it to do well." She turned towards the set, and Nathan fell into step beside her.

"You look tired."

"I am. We all are. The edits have been a lot of work. Just wait until you see it, which of course you won't until after the show's done. But keep on doing what you've been doing. You're a great first *Bachelor on Board*."

"I won't be a bachelor for too much longer if you have your way." He chuckled, and his gaze shifted to the small gaggle of women huddled around the fire, no doubt snitching about his absence.

"How long until the key ceremony?"

"Soon. I hope Jason hasn't ruined the mood for you."

"No, I'm good." He stood with her for a companionable moment before he took a deep breath and strode back into the fray. He playfully grabbed Sienna from behind and laughed when she took his hand and led him into the darkness beyond the flames. Amber listened to their whispered words, and Sienna's delighted giggles, but refused to watch. She rested her head on her arms on the wooden fence of the corral and stared at the moon, heavy and full.

Keep your eye on what's important, she lectured herself. You can do this. You might be attracted to Nathan. You might even have forgiven him—almost—for his adolescent behaviour, but you don't love him. Love? What was it anyway? Not this romantic fluff she'd created for the television world, although this was part of it. What girl didn't want to be wooed? Roses and champagne had their place, and it was an important place, but love? She listened to Nathan's murmured words and Sienna's giggle, and the sound lacerated.

Jealousy, cold and sharp.

But every woman around that circle of fire felt the same way. Every one of them felt that talon to her heart when Nathan took one or another of them away from the group. Love grew from chemistry and attraction, but how did it become more, and how was she to portray that on national television? How could she convince the audience that Nathan was truly in love? Love wasn't rational or sensible or even logical. Had Nathan already fallen in love with one of these women, but was hiding his true feelings until it was time to single her out? Dan fell hard and fast for Christina at first sight, and now they were to marry. Was it just a matter of timing, like musical chairs? Nathan had said that the time was right and so had every woman who'd signed up for the show. But need and want and love were three different things, and two out of three wasn't enough.

A barrage of cicadas reached a deafening crescendo, and she took a deep breath of the earthy air. Hell. She wanted Nathan to fall in love, and she needed the audience to believe it. A horse could be led to water... but love was a different beast.

Chapter Eight

Bachelor on Board. Already WED.

    Amber stood in a Darwin newsagency and the headline screamed at her from the cover of a popular women's magazine. Her heart bounced like a pin ball in her chest, and her breath snagged. What rubbish was this? Nathan couldn't be married already. It made no sense. Black curses rang in her ears. She'd sue the magazine editor from here to Hades. And death wasn't good enough for Nathan if it was true. Betrayal tasted bitter on her tongue and sickness stirred in her stomach. She snatched up the offending piece of melodrama and flipped to the exposè on page three.

She fought the spinning sensation. He couldn't have done this to her. She'd look like the worst kind of fool. More stupid than in high school. Tears stung behind her eyelids.

Nathan had signed a contract... Dan had signed a contract. *It's not what you think. It can't be, and if it is, you'll deal with it.*

She opened her eyes and there was Dan in a tuxedo with Christina on his arm, dressed to the nines in a wedding gown. Relief whooshed through her, leaving her light-headed and dizzy. Not Nathan. Dan. Of course it was Dan. But how had the press found out? Nathan stood beside him, gorgeous in a black tux. *Always the best man and never the groom? Not when the best man steps into the groom's empty shoes! Nathan Moretti. The runner-up star of Bachelor on Board.*

Nathan was the best man. Of course, they were close mates, but how had this gotten out? Amber devoured every word before closing the damn thing and adding it to her pile of purchases. Fury enveloped her like flame. This shouldn't have happened. Runner-up bachelor didn't have the same ring to it, and she'd worked hard to keep Nathan's identity a mystery. The television promos had built him up to be someone special, someone every woman would give a vital part of their anatomy to love. And now, this trashy magazine had stolen her thunder and taken the wind out of her sails.

Amber stormed back towards the girls. They'd stopped for supplies before they motored along the Kimberley coast towards Broome. She was torn between her need to speak with Nathan, and her need to cool down before she did so. The last thing she needed was Ron on her case. And wouldn't Jason gloat over the negative implications for viewer engagement with Nathan. Someone had sold Dan's story to the magazine, selling her out in the process. Who would gain from that? Jason? But how could he have known about Dan?

Amber approached the taxi rank where Cassie waited with six glamorously dressed women. Catherine, Mia, Juliette, Rebecca, Nina—the clumsy zoologist with her short pixie hair-cut—and Sienna, who with her dancer's body stood out from the rest. Cassie caught Amber's glare and rushed towards her. Amber raised the magazine cover for her to see and flicked to the photos inside.

"Oh, no. How could this have happened? Dan and Christina have confidentiality clauses in their contracts."

"Since when has this magazine had its facts straight?" Amber blasted. "These are lined up like soldiers at attention. Someone gave them the scoop." Her thoughts swung back to the night Jason crashed their outback shindig.

"Nina." She drew the young woman aside. "The other night when we were at the bush dance, you spoke with someone from the network. Jason Berringer. Did he ask you any questions about the show?"

"He was really interested in why I wanted to be part of the show. I mentioned I was sent home when things didn't click with Dan, but that I got a second chance when Nate came onboard, and that I had a better connection with him. I'm sorry if I shouldn't have. I was so thrilled for Christina because she and I got along well, and I assumed it was okay to talk about it because he was from the network."

"He's a snake in the grass and can't be trusted, and *you* have a nondisclosure clause in your contract." Amber did her best to convince herself that this could be fixed. Somehow. A cab pulled up, and she lowered herself into the back seat with the magazine on her knee, her gaze pinned to the headline.

"The girls are taking the one behind us." Cassie settled in beside Amber, her face pale. "Will this create a problem for the premiere tonight?"

"I'm not sure." Amber groaned. "Jason's responsible for this. I know it. And it isn't the work of last week, although that no doubt helped. He's been keeping tabs on me." She didn't trust herself when it came to men. Hormones messed with her brain and made her a fool.

"Professional jealousy is a bitch but take it as a compliment and keep doing what you're doing. Ignore him. If this is his worst, it could well backfire."

"You're right." Amber reached for her bottle of water and

took a sip. "Let's keep working. We have a date with the Kimberley, and it's the perfect place for romance." Her body felt rigid, her bones locked together. She was hot. Hot from the inside out. Moisture beaded on her upper lip, and her molars ground against each other. Her breath came in short, aggressive puffs. Damn, Jason.

The cruise from Darwin to Cape Leveque took several days, but the Kimberley coastline was better than perfect, it was stunning. Amber settled herself in the main dining room across from Cassie and sipped a cup of tea, letting the hum of the girls' conversations and the vibration of the cruising engines unkink some of the knots that twisted inside her.

"Cape Leveque sounds lovely, doesn't it?" Cassie enthused beside her. "We were lucky to get in at Kooljaman Resort."

"Yes, but the dates don't quite work. I think we'll travel from Cape Leveque to Broome via seaplane, and take in the Horizontal Falls, which can only be seen by air. Then we'll set the group date at a pearl farm outside of Broome."

"With a camel ride along Cable Beach for the individual date, and some footage at the resort."

"Then back to Cape Leveque by four-wheel drive for the rest of the filming. Being October, we should have the beach to ourselves." Amber held up her crossed fingers.

Cassie drained her cup. "The premier went really well. That magazine article didn't do us any harm—there's no such thing as bad publicity."

"I think Nathan has enough charm to capture the public's interest despite being portrayed as the runner-up instead of the main game." Amber hoped so, because she wanted Nathan to touch every woman out there, single or otherwise. The knife that seemed to reside permanently in her midriff shifted, and she screwed up her face. Nathan was out of bounds, off limits, and he'd hurt her enough for one lifetime.

"You're doing a great job, Am." Cassie reached out to touch her hand.

"We're all doing a great job. The show is the best we've ever made."

The Willie Creek pearl farm was about forty kilometres out of Broome, and Nathan went through the motions of the group date. Any other man would have been in heaven. Six women, all gorgeous, all smart, and all vying for his attention in a place that was as close to paradise as any he'd seen—but the woman he wanted was the one in the periphery of his vision. She stood on the dock in denim shorts and flip flops, a loose shirt over her singlet top. Her hair was caught up in a ponytail and pulled through her cap. She had a bottle of water in one hand, and she gesticulated with the other to get her point across.

"You still have feelings for her." A female voice, close to his ear. He turned to find Cassie beside him.

"We have a history," he replied carefully.

"She mentioned something about a bet and being the laughingstock of her school?"

"We were teenagers." He shrugged. "You remember how intense and confusing love can be at that age." Love, he'd used the word love? Oh crap. In hindsight, after a lot of thought and reflection, he'd realised his feelings for Amber had been as close to love as any he'd felt for any woman. Lust, definitely. Care? He'd cared. He'd been mortified when the rumours had circulated like wildfire. But trust? He hadn't trusted *her* feelings. He'd found it impossible to believe she could love him. He'd loved and ached and wanted but feared. Gutless was what he'd truly been. When it came to Amber and his feelings for her, he found himself tied in a tangle. He didn't blame her. He'd hurt her. He had a better understanding of that now. He'd hurt her more than she'd hurt him, if that was possible.

"True love doesn't unfold in a tidy, linear way," Cassie reflected. "What are you going to do about it?"

"I don't know. I'm contracted to find love on the show, but… "

"But the producer is not one of the contestants." She lifted her sunglasses and held his gaze. "Hmmm. We have a problem."

"I owe it to Amber to make her show a success, and I want her to shine. She needs me to select one of the contestants, and I need a wife." Not love. The words echoed in his head. Why not? Did he *still* believe he wasn't worthy of love? No. Yes. Was he afraid? Yes. He was afraid he was like his father. Incapable of loving one woman for always. The fact that he had feelings of a kind for each and every one of these women—even more so for Amber—meant his feelings were a sham and couldn't be trusted. Amber deserved to be loved. Completely. And truly. And forever. Every single one of these women deserved to be loved that way. Was he even capable of loving a woman forever, or was he too much like his father? He had his father's genes. His father's blood ran in his veins. He couldn't trust himself not to hurt her again. But he couldn't say he didn't want her. Or need her. Or love her.

"Leave it with me. I've been working on a plan."

"I can't let her down, Cassie. I won't. Not again." He said it with conviction. A conviction he felt all the way to his toes. And that meant turning his attention to the six remaining women in their itsy-bitsy bikinis. Their bodies were lithe and tanned and beautiful. A feast for a man's eyes, yet his drifted back to Amber. She sat on the edge of the small pier, her legs dangling over the water. She was deep in discussion with the director of photography, and Nate could see the way the man angled his body towards her. She laughed and the sound danced across the warm salty air. Infectious. Delightful. There was something about her. There always had been. It cut to his core, sliced through his doubts and buried itself like an arrow in his heart. Maybe it was her vulnerability, wrapped as it was in layers of strength. Or maybe it was her country soul and generosity of spirit. Her passion. Her joy. He didn't know, but he did know she affected him. More than he'd like. More than a woman should.

"No, you can't let her down and you won't." Cassie turned away, her attention on the boat motoring towards them. Nate gathered his things and shook the fancy from his thoughts. Catherine sauntered over and gave him a coy smile, her gaze capturing his. Brown eyes. Deeply warm.

"What did you think of the pearl farm?" Her tone was a purr. The cameras were there, never far away, always ready to capture a casual moment with a contestant.

"Who would have guessed that oysters could be seeded?"

"I think pearls are beautiful." She reached for her purchase, a single pearl on a leather necklace. "Look how luminous it is. Isn't it fascinating that it's formed by an oyster because of an irritating grain of sand?"

"Nature works in mysterious ways." Nathan helped her onto the motorboat that would take them back to Broome. They settled themselves into their seats, and the other girls joined them in a somewhat rowdy gathering after a brilliant day out and a sumptuous lunch cruise. Nate adjusted his sunglasses and gazed out at the incredible azure of the water and the pristine white of the sand beneath.

"It's stunning here, isn't it?" Catherine murmured next to him. The boat picked up speed and the breeze was a welcome relief from the warmth of the sun. Catherine's hair flew out behind her, and Nate couldn't stop the feeling of well-being. How long had it been since he'd had a holiday? He couldn't remember. The thrill of the trip was amplified when one of the staff called out and pointed to a pod of whales breaching not far from the boat's side. They all gasped with the thrill of watching the huge beasts so close they seemed to be playing with them. Nate observed Amber's animated face and couldn't remember when he'd gotten such joy from watching another person's excitement. She turned and her gaze snagged with his… and her cheeks flushed pink. He smiled and she smiled back, and the power of it sucked the oxygen from the air. Her sea-green eyes stole his breath. He physically couldn't drag his gaze from hers and the stunning paradise around them ceased to exist.

"Whales, Nate," she whispered, her voice in his ear.

"Incredible." And he wasn't referring to the enormous mammals playing in the waves. It was then that he realised there was only one woman for him, and she was the one woman he couldn't have. They had a history, and it may have been brief, but one taste of Morticia Reed and a man was bewitched. For life it seemed.

"Did you get that?" Cassie demanded.

"I did," agreed John, one of the top camera guys. "You were right. We've caught some great moments over the past couple of weeks."

"I want a camera on them at all times. Catch every secret

glance. Every quiet communication. At Cape Leveque, I'll organise a surprise date on the beach, a fire, apparent solitude. Amber will possibly never forgive me, but if what I have in mind works, we'll create some great TV. Better than great. I want you and the camera concealed. I don't want her to know you're filming. Let's keep this between us."

"I'm not sure I like it. I feel like we're invading her privacy." He rubbed his eyes, heavy with fatigue. "Amber would be within her rights to have me fired, and I like my job. This is outside the brief."

"True, but it's *me* she'll have fired, because I gave you the directive, but hopefully she'll be eternally grateful and forgive us."

"She's not going to like it when she sees the footage in edits," John persisted

"She's not going to see them until she needs to. I'll polish them and incorporate them into a second tape, and she can do with that what she sees fit. One copy. Her choice. The finale will be filmed and done, well before those scenes are screened to the public. If I'm wrong and this doesn't pan out, she can hold them back. If it does pan out, these will be gold, and she'll thank us forever." Fingers crossed, she thought. Hell, she should cross every limb in her body. It was a big risk, but she couldn't stand by and watch the love of Amber's life marry another woman because of a stupid contract and a promise that was misguided at best. She'd seen the change in her best friend. Amber wanted Nate as much as Nate wanted her, and if there was a way to capture the audience's sympathy and get them together? She'd take it. She'd risk it.

"Are you crazy, Cassie? This is *Amber* we're talking about." John raked his hands through his hair, dragging it away from his face.

"She's my best friend in the world, and I have her best interests at heart. I promise you that." Cassie's voice was raw with emotion.

"Alright, but it's your head on the chopping block. I'm following orders."

"I know, but I have a feeling about this. Trust me." It would work out. It had to.

It was a two-hundred-kilometre trek back to Cape Leveque on the Dampier Peninsula, and they travelled via four-wheel drive convoy. The terracotta-coloured road snaked through low-lying vegetation and contrasted vividly with the azure blue of the sky. Amber was shaken from the endless corrugations, but she loved the colours and the vast wilderness that stretched for miles. After a trip of nearly three hours, they arrived at the Cape.

"What's next?" Nate asked, his aviator sunglasses reflecting back the rugged scenery and the incredible colour around them.

"First, we get our accommodation sorted," Amber said. "Then *we* get back to work, and *you* get to relax and enjoy your holiday with six gorgeous women."

"That's some office you have going." He surveyed the scenery.

The eco-resort rested almost invisibly against the spectacular coastline in front of them. There were Safari tents—sophisticated structures on stilts—nestled into the red cliffs and wilderness, overlooking the deserted beach and the ocean. Amber gazed out to the sleek superyacht moored off the coast. It was nice to be back on solid ground, but she'd loved the spectacular sights of the Kimberley and the archipelago that dotted the coastline. A board walk led from the accommodation towards a lighthouse and the other side of the cape, and the beach had powdery white sand, broken here and there by outcrops of red rock.

"Let's hope there aren't any frogs in the toilets." Nathan laughed.

"You and me both," Amber agreed. "I couldn't handle any more hysterics, although I'm pretty sure there'll be plenty of wildlife here, too." Juliette's screams the night before had added some spice to the footage of the contestants relaxing with Nathan around the pool at the Cable Beach resort. Amber had run to find a lime-green frog, the size of her palm looking up at her from his watery happy place. With the exception of Nina, who'd taken it in her stride, the others had been horrified.

"You must have missed, Niko," she said as they made their way to the small resort office.

"I did, but he wouldn't have liked the flight or the long drive, and I'm sure he would have gone crazy at the camels."

"Tonight, we'll have a big fire on the beach, and he can join us there. We'll cook the fish we're going to catch today." Her attention shifted to the receptionist. The resort was owned and run by the local indigenous people. She dealt with the formalities and organised the room allocations then turned to the rest of the group. "We'll meet back here in fifteen minutes. Get settled and dress for a fishing trip. Remember your sunscreen and hats," she said. "Then we'll have a quick cup of tea and head off."

Amber and Cassie headed to their shared accommodation. It was an amazing space, and one entire canvas wall opened to the Indian Ocean. It was right on the beach and the sound of the waves was a steady throb. Cassie threw herself back on the large king-sized bed, and Amber laughed. "There's no time for relaxing, Miss Shaw. We have work to do."

"Do you believe this scenery? It's stunning. This place is perfect for romance. They'll have a major influx of visitors after the show goes to air."

"A win-win of the best possible kind," Amber agreed.

"Yes." Cassie grinned. "Let's get back to work."

The boat had an outboard motor and was big enough to transport them all around the islands. Their indigenous guide, Jarli, was very knowledgeable. The stories and fables he shared about the various islands and rocky outcrops made for some interesting snippets of TV, and the sight of the girls and Nathan with their long bamboo fishing poles reeling in their catch was engaging. Nathan's tanned back rippled with muscle. He helped the girls land their fish and, damn it, he'd win the heart of every woman on the planet. Amber resigned herself to the bone-gripping misery she'd created for herself in the middle of paradise. Every one of the contestants flushed with desire when he was close. And he was close. He stood behind Sienna and helped her reel in a massive barramundi, his arms around her, his hands over hers. Their excitement was visible, and Sienna glowed with pleasure when he congratulated her on her success.

"Dinner," he said with a grin at Amber, and she couldn't help but smile back. His joy was infectious, and the day was perfect, as much as it could be, watching Nathan flirt with the girls, until Nina's clumsiness caused her to trip on a rope and fall into the water. Swimming was not her forte either, it seemed, but Nathan was quick to dive in after her. She didn't make his job easy and her awkward attempts to keep her face above

132

water forced them both further from the boat.

With everyone's attention on Nathan and Nina, they didn't immediately see the dark shape that approached in the pristine water. Amber noticed it first and with a spike of fear, spoke calmly but firmly into the headpiece.

"Nate, I need you both back on the boat. Now."

Nate stopped teasing Nina and looked around, his tanned face draining of colour when he saw the fin break the surface. He froze and Nina screamed. The fin disappeared under the surface of the water, and Amber wanted to shriek into the microphone. Instead, she held a tight leash on her own fear and spoke with false certainty.

"Nate, you need to swim to the boat." *Now,* she shrieked inside her head. *Now.*

Jarli reached for the donut shaped life-saving device and threw it towards them. It floated close, so close, but neither Nina nor Nathan reached for it.

"Nate, take hold of the lifebuoy. Please." She leaned so far over the side of the boat she nearly fell in with them.

"Nate." She captured his gaze and spoke softly like she would to a spooked horse. "You're fine. You just need to get out of the water. Here." She leaned out and stretched her hand towards him. The dark shape flashed in the water below and she all but shrieked with panic. "Please, Nate. You need to get on to the boat."

"No," he whispered. "We can't move. We have to stay still. Quiet."

Amber's heart thudded like a jackhammer in her chest.

Jarli studied the intruder and called out in broken English. "It's okay. It's a sandbar shark. It won't hurt you." He grabbed a bleeding fish from the deck and threw it a good distance from the boat. The shape flashed in the water and shot towards the bait. Nathan took the opportunity and moved slowly, slowly towards the vessel.

"Get them out, get them out." Amber's voice was hoarse. She was beyond terrified as she watched the shark devour the barramundi in a cloud of crimson and swishing tail. She reached for Nathan's hand and with help from the others, managed to pull them both from the water before the shark circled back towards them. Jarli threw another fish, and its fin flashed in the sun as it snatched the offering and dived into the depths.

"It's a sandbar shark and a beauty at that. Three metres at least. She came for the fish. I've never heard of one attacking a human," Jarli assured them.

Nathan collapsed on the floor of the boat and leaned back against one of the seats. His face was whiter than Nina's bikini. Amber crouched beside him. "You're both safe, Nate. It's okay. You're safe."

He took long, slow breaths, and she saw the grip of fear in his taut muscles and his tightly clenched eyes. "You saved Nina from drowning." She opened a fresh bottle of water. "Here. Have a sip."

"I'm fine," he growled. "I'm okay."

Amber turned to check on Nina. The girls had gathered around her in a concerned group, and someone had produced a towel and wrapped it around her shoulders.

She stepped unsteadily towards Nathan. "Thank you, Nate. I'm so clumsy. I don't know how I managed to end up in the water."

"We're going to have to tie you down," Amber teased, although the little mishap had made for some exciting footage.

Perhaps too exciting, she thought, glancing down at Nate. Her hand rested on his shoulder and tension raged in the muscle beneath her touch. She sheltered him from the concerned glances of the other girls.

"He's fine," she assured Nina. "He just needs a moment to recover from the fright. Perhaps you should sit down, too. You still look a bit shaken." Amber turned her concerned gaze back to Nate. His head was tipped back, and he stared up at the sky. She could see his struggle to regain his composure and the crazy thump of his pulse in the taut skin of his throat. He'd been past terrified. She'd been terrified herself. If the shark had attacked? The thought left her light-headed. "Jarli, maybe we should go in."

"I'm fine." Nate wiped the wetness from his face with a towel. His skin had regained some colour. "Nina says she's fine. We need fish for dinner. Let's stick with the schedule."

"You don't have to." Amber's voice softened. "We can head back. You could lie down for a while."

"I'm fine. Don't we have a picnic lunch or something?"

Trust a male to think of food at a time like this. "We do." She turned to the others and said in a louder voice, "Let's have lunch. There's wine and fresh bread. Cheese. Dips. Salad." And champagne. For once in her life, she would break her own rules and have a glass. The adrenalin that had kept her focused and reactive drained from her body, and she sat with a thump. Hell. She'd been so scared. Rogue thoughts raced through her head. Thoughts she had no right thinking. Thank God Nathan was okay. And not because her show would have taken a terrible turn for the worse had her lead man been eaten by a shark, but because the thought of losing him... Stupid, stupid woman. What had she done? She had feelings for him?

She had feelings for him, and she had to watch him fall in love with another woman.

"Nate asked for some time to meet with you before the key ceremony tonight," Cassie said during a short break between the group date and the individual date.

Amber turned to her in confusion. "He did? Is there a problem?"

"Not that I'm aware of."

She looked smug and Amber's heart skipped a beat. "I'm surprised he chose Nina for the one-on-one. We'll have to be on guard. A stroll along the beach should be okay—hopefully—but champagne, cheese, chocolate, and strawberries, at the top of the lighthouse? All those stairs. Walking up. Walking down!" Amber broke out in a sweat at the thought.

"With views stretching in three hundred and sixty degrees around them, and an intimate space for talking and getting to know each other."

Amber refused to entertain the sharp stab of envy. She dropped her gaze to the schedule in front of her and frowned. "We don't have much time between the individual date and the barbecue dinner on the beach. I guess there's time if it's important. Nate has to let two girls go tonight." She'd organised a small plane to pick them up in the morning and the necessary transfers for their trip back to Sydney. "I'm glad it's not me who has to choose. They're all terrific women."

Stay busy, she lectured herself. Too busy to think beyond the stress of the next five minutes. One step at a time until the blissful TV moment when he proposed to the woman of his dreams on national television. And he would propose because he needed a wife. Why hadn't she asked him more about that?

Why the rush? Why now?

Why all the questions, she growled at herself. What did she care beyond the fact that it suited her purpose right down to the sun-kissed, red-coloured, ancient ground?

"I've created some time. Here." Cassie pointed to their schedule. "Besides, we can get some footage of the girls chatting about their trip to the Kimberley, and their hopes for the home visits. Their fears regarding who will stay and who will go. We'll try to capture their quiet talk. With Nathan missing, that should be interesting. There's sure to be lots of backchat."

"Okay, but is there something wrong? Did he mention what it was about? I hope he doesn't want to pull out." Just the thought was enough to give her heart palpitations. No. He was contracted to stay until he took a ring box from his pocket. It would be fine. She could do this. *Breathe in. Breathe out.* He wouldn't let her down. Would he?

"No, nothing like that. He mentioned how important it was for the show to be a success. He wants that for you."

"He wants that for himself." Amber clung to her old hurt like a worry stone, but Cassie was right. He'd changed and he did want the show to be a success, but for the show to be a success... he had to marry one of the contestants. It was for the best, she consoled herself. When it came to Nate, the stars were not aligned. So, she had feelings for him—feelings rooted in her teenage crush—and he needed a wife. And that was the crux of it. He wasn't looking for love, and she wouldn't accept anything less.

Chapter Nine

"Are you sure this thing's road-worthy?" Amber asked through the open window when Nate drew up in front of her in a battered four-wheel drive. She was wearing a short skirt and a pink singlet, along with casual runners. It seemed less than wise to walk around in flip flops in the wilderness of the outback. The size of the goanna they'd seen on the boardwalk as they'd made their way back from the lighthouse had confirmed it. This was not downtown Sydney.

"Yes, and we're going for a drive." He got out and strode around to the passenger door. "It's not every day we get to steal a moment away from the madding crowd, and I have it on very good authority there's a gem of a beach not ten minutes down the road that's well worth a visit."

"Wouldn't you rather rest after your excitement today?"

"No, but thanks for caring." He grinned, and she couldn't help but smile back because well, his enthusiasm was infectious. He opened the dented door for her to get into the passenger seat and waited while she climbed in. He skirted the front of the vehicle and lowered himself into the worn leather seat beside her.

"Alright, Romeo. Let's get on with this. What did you want to discuss with me?"

"The perfect date."

"You'd like us to squeeze in another date with one of the girls before the home visits?" That would be a struggle. He cranked the air conditioning, and the fan was loud in the too-small space between them, but the rush of air on her hot skin was very welcome. Hell, why had she agreed to this? The last thing she needed was to spend time with Nathan, who turned casual shorts and a short-sleeved shirt into an indictable offence. She supposed a discussion regarding his feelings for the contestants came within the brief of her job, but truly, being his confidante was beyond difficult.

"I think every woman should experience the perfect date, don't you?" He revved the motor and the vehicle bumped across the rough corrugations on the road, which was more like a red dust bowl punctuated by horizontal ruts than a bona fide road.

"Isn't that what we've aimed for, over and over?" Amber said with confusion. "Did you enjoy your date with Nina?"

"Did I survive my date with Nina might be a more appropriate question. Incredibly, I did. We managed to climb to the top of the lighthouse and down again without mishap. A small miracle. That woman should come with a health warning."

"You're not kidding. I've never been more terrified than I was today when I saw that shark. It was huge. I could barely speak. How did you know not to move?"

"I froze with fear. I was terrified." He slammed through the gears, and the gearbox made a shrieking sound.

Amber cringed. Hopefully, they wouldn't end up stranded God-knew-where. There was probably only an hour or so of daylight left, and she wanted to see the sun set over the western beach. "I've never seen anyone turn so pale."

"I thought I was dead." His knuckles whitened on the steering wheel.

"I'm glad you're not." Amber's tone was husky, and her heart did a funny flip flop in her chest. The air between them grew thick with skin-prickling awareness. Damn it. The yearning in her soul was right there, and she fought to disguise it. "I can't afford to lose another lead man," she quipped. "The rescheduling would be a nightmare."

Nate sat in silence, his aviator glasses hiding his eyes as the vehicle shuddered over the rough terrain. She couldn't know what he was thinking, but she hoped she'd covered her gaffe. They turned into a roughly hewn track which headed west towards the beach. There was a small turning area and, except for evidence of tyre tracks on the road, there wasn't a soul to be seen. "It really is remote here, isn't it?" Apprehension crawled over her skin. They were alone. Together. With no one around.

"Come on." He cut the engine and opened the door. "This beach is supposed to be something special." He waited for her to catch up and directed her to a narrow track through the vegetation.

Amber glanced around. "I hope there aren't any goannas about. Those things are huge."

"We'll be fine," he assured her and took her hand. She shouldn't have let him. She should have snatched it back immediately, but she hesitated for the smallest moment and then the smooth comfort of his palm against hers stirred something deep inside her, and she was lost to everything except for his touch and his scent and the memories that waylaid her.

They burst from the scrub onto a small rocky cliff and then

140

stepped down onto the sand. Amber kicked off her runners and let her toes sink into the powdery softness. "How good is this sand? And look at the colour of the water. It's amazing."

"Let's go for a walk, and we can talk." He drew her into the shallows and the warm water splashed over their feet. The waves created a soothing, primal beat, and the sky spread before them—pink, orange and red—but Amber's attention was on the warmth of Nate's hand and the thud of her heart in her chest.

"What's on your mind?" Amber cursed her own weakness. Let go of his hand. Let go of his hand. She couldn't think of anything but the mesmerising connection, and the sensations that eddied from her hand to that part of her that yearned and wanted and physically ached.

"Our close call with the shark today reminded me that life's short. I want to share with you what happened after I left school that changed everything."

"Besides Bethany's death and your parents breaking up, and Isabella being sick? There's more?"

"Yes. You'll remember that I loved to surf. Dan and I used to surf together at every opportunity."

Amber nodded. How could she have forgotten? He'd worn a shark's tooth on a piece of leather around his neck. He'd been tanned and fit and loved the beach and the waves. After they'd broken up, she'd sat and stared at the surf for hours, feeling somehow more connected to him there. He'd been such a part of her soul that their break-up had left her torn inside, and it was a part of her that had never healed. She would do well to remember the agony of it. She wanted and she yearned, but she couldn't have. The timing had been wrong, and it was still wrong. She went to slip her hand from his, but his grip tightened and held hers close.

"Am, please. This is difficult."

Amber stopped fighting and the tension in his hand eased.

"It was early morning and the sun had just risen when we hit the water. It was warm, towards the end of the summer holidays. Dan and I loved the power of the ocean, the feel of catching a wave and riding it like gladiators. But that day, something big rose out of the barrel of the wave and there was nothing I could do. A shark, and a big bastard white pointer at that. Its teeth savaged my board and missed my foot by I don't know how much. It flipped me into the surf and tossed me like a toy. I was disoriented—I didn't know which way was up—and I must have taken in a mouthful of water, because my chest felt like it was going to burst. I thought I was dead, and I would have been except for Dan. He should have got the hell away, but instead, he came to help. He grabbed me and pulled me up onto his board, but the bastard came back and took another swipe. Dan took the worst of it—his leg was mashed. I got mad at the thing and yelled my lungs free of water. I punched it full in the face. I got Dan on the board and paddled like there was no tomorrow.

Somehow, we got to shore but I thought Dan was going to die, he was bleeding so badly. Someone on the beach called an ambulance, and I held a towel to his leg. My God, Amber, I was so afraid, and my selfish, miserable life flashed before my eyes. I knew then and there that if Dan lived, if Dan survived, I would never take my life for granted again. I would make it count. I would be humble. I would be grateful."

Amber didn't realise she was crying until Nate stopped walking and pulled her towards him. He gently wiped the tears from her face, his blue gaze filled with emotion, and drew her close to his chest. They stood for a long time, just holding each other, the moment too perfect to spoil. The warm ocean waves splashed over their feet, only to drain away and reach for them again.

"Dan saved your life, and you saved his." She spoke into the warmth of his chest."

"Yes," he agreed. "We both grew up that day, and I realised later that my father never has. His pleasure and his ego have always come first. Even when Bella was sick, so sick she nearly died, he wasn't there. He was too self-involved, too egotistical to look beyond his own needs and those of his self-serving wife. I find it sad that he doesn't know how much he's missed. I don't want to be like him. I vowed I would live my life differently."

"I understand now." Her voice was quiet, but it thrummed with all that she felt. "Your fear at the aquarium and in the ocean today. You were beyond terrified."

"It took me a long time to get back into the surf. Even now, I won't go out on my board. I'll swim in the waves, but the danger is there, and I find it hard to block out. Before, surfing was an escape. From Mum and Dad fighting. From Dad's infidelity. From life. But now I know that life can be over in the blink of an eye. And so too, does Dan.

"So that's why he couldn't go through with the show once he found Christina," Amber nodded with a flash of understanding. "You did this for Dan, and now I get what you owed him, and why you stepped in for him when he needed to step out." She stopped and stared up at Nate's blue eyes, so crystal clear, so brilliant against the honey tanned skin of his face—at the gorgeous dimples that creased his cheeks, the delicious curve of his lips. Dark stubble shadowed the square line of his jaw. Her heart beat hard and fast. She saw his half smile and the flash of his teeth. Her hand lifted of its own volition and cradled the side of his face for even though he wasn't hers, once upon a time he had been, and her body knew it and there was magic in that. "Do you truly want to find love and marry one of these girls, or are you sacrificing your own life in return for Dan's? You don't need to do that. Not for him. Not for me." Hell. What was she saying? What the hell was she saying?

"I do want to marry. I need to marry, but quite frankly, I'm not even sure I know what love is." He looked down at her and the sadness in his eyes healed scars she'd thought would never mend.

"I treated you badly, and I don't expect your forgiveness. My behaviour was unforgiveable and then there was Bethany. I've learned it's best to keep my relationships short and sweet. I don't want to hurt anyone the way my father hurt my mother, and my track record isn't great, but equally, I don't want to gift my hard-earned fortune to my stepmother. My grandfather made it a condition in his will, that in order to inherit the family business, I have to marry. If my father dies before I marry, his wife gets the lot. Hence my rush. My father whittled away my grandfather's fortune, and *I've* worked hard to build the business back to what it was. My stepmother will drop my father faster than she can max out her credit card when the money runs out. She'll finally see him for the middle-aged, man-child that he is. And he'll finally see her for the money-grabbing, gold-digger that she is."

"So why didn't you just marry one of your lady-friends?" Amber challenged him.

"Because most of them were in the market for a wealthy husband, and I couldn't bear a relationship like my father's. I hope one of these women will like me enough to marry me *and* sign a prenuptial agreement.''

Amber's heart banged against her ribs as her mind tripped to the final scene of her show. To Nate down on his knee. To the proposal—the diamond ring—but first allow my lawyer to explain the terms of our business arrangement and please sign here on the dotted line? I promise to love you for now, until someone better comes along? She took a deep breath and stared into the blue, blue depths of his eyes, a wave of emotion crashing over her. This was the man she'd loved—she loved—with every pore, every cell, every breath, and he was telling her he wasn't capable of love or trust? He wanted a wife to protect his millions?

How could she have fallen in love with someone so incapable of loving her back? Or was he wrong? She thought back to the loving reassurance her grammy had given her when she'd been so heartbroken. What if Grammy hadn't been there, promising love was worth the struggle, the pain, the hurt, the longing? Surely, Nate was capable of love—look at him with Niko—but fear kept him from wanting to believe it. Just like fear kept him from surfing. He'd been terribly hurt by his father. She saw that now and it meant everything.

She lowered her gaze to the firm flesh of his lips and opened herself to the heady pull of the magic that shimmered there. Spellbound, she narrowed the distance, her breath mingling with his, her mind loud with wishes, her body buzzing with anticipation. She waited, a hair's breadth from what she wanted to take—to give—and he pounced, hungry for what she offered.

Time fell away and the anger, the hurt, the betrayal was gone, washed away by the silky warmth of the waves at their feet, leaving only desire, the heavy pull of it in her veins, the urgency of it in her ears.

He tasted and soothed and stoked the fire he found there, and she feasted in return, engulfed by the flames he roused. His touch was firm on her back, pulling her close, so close that she felt his hardness against her, but it was his kiss that took the strength from her legs and left her light-headed with all that she craved. Firm and furious, soft and delicious, hungry, sad, tender and more. There was the ebb and flow of the waves, the feel of warm, firm muscle beneath the smooth fabric of his shirt, the slide of her hand through his hair. The musky, citrusy, freshness of his skin, and the salty tang of the ocean.

He groaned as he tasted, and the rhythm of what pounded between them was more primal than the splash and pull of the waves at their feet. Amber could no more have pulled herself back from the brink than she could have stopped her next erratic breath.

Desire was a demand in her head and reason was so far distant it didn't exist.

Time was a liquid thing. She didn't know how long they stood, or when they no longer fought the drag of gravity but instead found themselves on the soft, powdery sand.

When Nate finally eased back, when her vision cleared, and she saw the answering bewilderment in his gaze, when she finally caught her breath and sought the horizon, the sun was a golden, fiery ball in a sea of reds and oranges. The cliffs behind them glowed and the sand around them was luminous with rosy light.

"Oh my God," she gasped. The world was on fire. Her body was on fire. What the hell had she done?

"Amber," he began.

"We need to get back." She struggled to her feet. The key

ceremony. She needed to get Nathan on set and soon.

"Cassie gave us a leave pass. Until nine." He lifted himself from the ground and took her hand in his, linking their fingers loosely. "You're so beautiful right now."

I'm so stupid right now. How had she thought this was a good idea? She hadn't thought. If she'd thought, she'd have known that one taste would never be enough. She wanted more. Already. She wanted to gorge herself stupid. Hell, she had gorged herself stupid.

"You're over-thinking it, Am. Let's just be in the moment. I have a picnic. Champagne."

"*My* perfect date," she said on a sigh. "You remembered." A deserted beach. Wilderness. The ocean. A picnic. Seclusion. "A fire on the beach? Marshmallows?"

"Just the two of us," he said with a grin.

"What about the key ceremony?"

"Cassie has it covered for now."

"How did you get her on side?" Cassie was a romantic at heart, but this couldn't go anywhere good.

"She wants you to be happy."

"I am happy right now, but in a few hours…I have to watch you give cabin keys to four gorgeous women who all want to take you home to meet their families. For better or worse, and I guess that includes a prenuptial agreement."

"Right now, I'm with *you,* and I couldn't think of any place I'd rather be."

He'd perfected the line. She'd heard him use it multiple times throughout the show.

"Okay, for old times' sake, let's get on with this." She couldn't help the grin. She was in paradise with her favourite man in the world, and it didn't matter how many women were waiting for him on another beach; he was hers for now.

"I'll be right back." He grinned, as excited as the schoolboy she'd fallen in love with, and he tore back the way they'd come. Amber stood like the rocky outcrops around her. Still. Serene. Steady. She'd live in the moment and pay for it later. For once, she'd gift herself this... A moment to remember. A moment to cherish. A moment she'd hold close. And when Nathan married the woman of his choice, she'd remember what was important and celebrate the success of her show.

Nate's face glowed in the twilight as he coaxed the flame to feed on the kindling and dried seaweed. It devoured them in a crackle and pop of sparks, before moving on with its golden tongue to taste the driftwood and logs. Amber couldn't stop the sense of well-being as the fire caught and flourished in the growing darkness. She sat on the silken sand and sipped champagne, the waves a comforting ebb and splash against the shore. Fresh barramundi rested in foil ready to roast on the coals, and Nate spread out a feast of cheese and crackers, olives, and dips. Twilight deepened around them and the navy ink of the sky was like velvet beneath the bejewelled glitter of the stars.

Nate settled himself beside her, and it was like the world narrowed to their own little patch of dancing light. The insects—so loud not moments before—quieted and Amber could hear the rapid thud of her pulse. Her gaze rested on the rose-tipped edge of the horizon, the colour snuffed by the darkness as she watched.

"It's still there, isn't it?" Nate spoke quietly and she felt his gaze on her face. "Attraction. Maybe more."

"I loved you." Sadness stalked her words. "I know it wasn't

like that for you, but it was for me, and I felt like a fool." No doubt tomorrow she would again.

"I don't know if what I felt for you was love, but I felt it strongly. I still do. We had something special, and I wish I'd appreciated it more at the time."

"Perhaps we did have something special." She refused to let the pain of the past spoil the magic of the moment.

"Do you think you could ever feel that way again?"

"I think love lasts forever whether we like it or not. When we gift our heart to someone, that part of us is given for always. Love doesn't know boundaries or conditions or even sense." Quite clearly, or she wouldn't be having this conversation. It was beyond stupid to confess what she'd felt for him all those years ago, but to suggest her feelings were still there? It was beyond madness. She didn't want what swirled between them as primal as the tide.

"Do you think you could ever forgive me and love me again?" The hope in his tone was beyond her capacity to resist.

"You are worthy of love, Nate. Your father doesn't define you. *You* define you. You decide what kind of person you're going to be. You're far from the person you were and you're far from the person your father is, but whether I love you or not—and I think I'll always love you—I don't think it's wise to revisit the past. I'm sorry, but I..." If only he knew how sorry she was... but she couldn't bear to lose him again. It was beyond crazy to encourage him. Hadn't he just told her he wasn't sure he could commit to one woman? Didn't he have six women waiting on tenterhooks? Better to remember what was important. Her career. Her professional reputation. She couldn't risk her heart again, not when he had the power to hurt her so deeply. "This show is important to me."

"Jason didn't deserve you either." Nate reached for her hand and took her heart. Desire fizzed and popped like champagne in her veins. She nearly gave in to the want and the need and the love she would always feel for him. But she wasn't a naïve teenager anymore. She was older and wiser, and she'd learned that her heart was worth protecting. She wouldn't fall for his engineering. She knew better than to trust the romance he'd woven around them. Hadn't she watched him weave his magic with one woman after another? No, she wasn't a fool. Not anymore.

"I respect you, and I would never ask for more than you're willing to give. This whole situation is a mess. I know what you're thinking. You've seen this scenario played out over and over, and no doubt spent hours editing and tweaking the footage." His tone was frustrated.

"I have," she agreed.

"Which makes it less real and harder to trust." He raked his free hand through his hair.

"Yes."

He drew her closer to him, and she closed her eyes to better savour the sensations that swamped her. Bitter pleasure. A stolen moment. If hearts could merge and be one, then she was sure she felt hers expand and shift within her chest. But of course, they couldn't, and she shook the foolish sentiment from her mind. Don't go backwards, she lectured herself. Move forward. Move onward.

She breathed him in and treasured the moment, storing every sensation in her memory. Her body yearned and her soul cried. His touch soothed. Murmured endearments rained against her hair. Fool's gold—so pretty, so sparkly. Unexpected, like a perfect shell or a milky pearl, but not hers. She knew better than to fall for it. His touch against her hair, his lips against her forehead… Wishes, wishes, whispering around her.

"Thank you for organising this. It really is lovely." Her resistance ebbed away with the magnetic pull of him.

"It is." He stroked her face, his big hand gentle against her skin, his touch leaving a trail of longing. "You're so beautiful."

"Nate, I…" What could she say that would make this less agonising? She wanted to believe attraction was enough, but it wasn't. She couldn't risk it. Not without sabotaging everything.

"You deserve way more than I can give," he said in a husky tone. "But that doesn't stop me from wanting you."

"You're contracted to find love with someone else." She sighed. "There's nowhere this can go, Nate, but I thank you for my perfect date and for a precious memory I'll treasure always."

"You're right. I want your show to be a success. You deserve that." He was silent for a long moment. "But to give you that, I have to let you go."

"I know." She almost wept, it hurt so much to say. For her show to succeed, she had to give up any chance of loving him. She steadied her gaze on the dancing flame, on the blue, blue heart of it and opened herself to the joy of being close to him. She sipped her champagne and leaned into the hard muscle of his chest. His arms encircled her and held her tight. She closed her eyes to better savour the moment, delicious and stolen. Later, she'd be strong. Later, she'd protect her heart.

"If you could use only one word to describe you, what would you choose?" Nate asked as they drove back to the resort, their vehicle banging over bone-jarring corrugations, their headlights illuminating an arch of red road.

"Passionate." Amber didn't need to think. "What about you? What word would you choose?"

"Responsible."

"I would have guessed Lothario."

"Once," he agreed.

"Perhaps you've overcompensated." She twisted in her seat to gaze at his profile in the glow of the dashboard light. "Life shouldn't be all about responsibility, although its important."

"Duty and discipline. Goals and aspirations. Contributions and causes." His expression was carefully controlled.

"What about family and friends?" Lovers, she thought in the quiet that followed.

"I work a lot." His voice was laced with fatigue.

"I'm passionate about my work, too," she said, her voice soft.

"I hadn't thought of it like that, but in truth it's a way of hiding from what's important." He turned towards her, emotion storming in his eyes.

"You've had some hard lessons, like all of us. That's what makes us grow."

His gaze held hers for a heart-stopping moment before shifting back to the road in front of them. "Yes, that's true." He fell into silence.

Amber yearned to reach out and comfort him. Tonight, the boundaries around her feelings had crumbled. To want Nathan was insanity. To love him was certifiable. And to see the hope and warmth in the eyes of six women she admired at the cocktail party tonight... She braced herself as the car lost traction in the sand and the engine shrieked in protest. She screamed and Nate reached out to protect her.

Chapter Ten

"Rebecca, Catherine, Mia and Nina." And then there were four, Amber thought. "Launceston, Perth, Melbourne and Queensland." She ticked the corresponding home visits off on her fingers. Cassie sat in the white leather chair on the other side of her desk, pen poised above a notebook. They were back in Sydney at the network office to work on the edits and the final phase of the show.

"I've organised flights to Maroochydore for this afternoon. Tomorrow we'll travel to Australia Zoo to see Nina. Then to her family in the evening," Cassie answered.

"We could fly to Launceston the morning after for Rebecca's home visit." Amber pondered the dates in front of her. "Grammy's funeral is at one o'clock so I could leave you to oversee Nate's date with Rebecca. She's organised a visit to Cataract Gorge and lunch cruising Launceston's riverfront precinct."

"Where's Nate's family?"

"In Sydney. So back here for the final two dates. It'll be intriguing to meet his mum." Amber lifted the takeaway cup to her lips. The rich, sweet scent of coffee soothed the ache in her chest. She would find Nate a wife, then she'd get him out of her mind and, more importantly, out of her heart.

She had an idea for a new project and if all went well with *Bachelor on Board*, she'd present it to Ron and see what he thought. Perhaps Jason had done her a favour. He'd given her an opportunity to exorcise Nate from her soul and the show was good. It was better than good. She'd spent two fifteen-hour days with the editor following their trip to Broome and the excitement still buzzed in her veins. Albeit in tango with Envy, not to mention Guilt and most brazen of all, Desire. She shook the whimsy from her thoughts.

Home visits. Stay busy. It was the only way to stop thinking and over-analysing and ruminating on what might have been, what could have been, or what would have been if she'd been filming *The Amazing Race* and Nate had been a contestant. Or not, because clearly, he wasn't the one for her. She took a sad sip of her latte.

"What about his dad? His parents are separated, aren't they?" Cassie had that look on her face, the sort that burrowed under a person's skin and imposed on their inner most thoughts.

"He'll want the lion's share of the footage to be with his mum."

"How did your meeting with Nate go the other night? Did he give you any idea about where his thoughts are headed?" Cassie asked with an innocent lift of her brows.

"No, not really." Amber's cheeks flushed with a rush of warmth as she thought back to their *date* on the beach.

"I have a good feeling about this, Am." Cassie took a sip of her coffee. "If he has us guessing, he'll keep the audience guessing right up until the last minute. Everyone will be arguing over their morning coffee about which contestant he should choose and no doubt everyone will have an opinion."

"I don't think he knows himself at this stage. Hopefully, the home visits will help him sort it out. A person's family is an important consideration. If a couple's upbringing is too different, that will impact on the way they raise their children." She hadn't thought of that. *Her* background couldn't be more different from Nate's. A relationship between them would never work—she pounded another nail into the already well-fixed lid on her coffin of hope. She should have left her feelings in the past. There was nothing clean about the bones of their relationship.

The sound of skittering paws made her jump, and her gaze shifted to the half-open doorway. Niko scooted through it, his tail wagging like a whip.

"Niko," she called, and he ran full pelt towards her and onto her lap, his front paws doing all kinds of wicked to her silk shirt. She didn't care.

"He misses you." Nate appeared in the doorway wearing jeans that hugged his hips and a black shirt... one of those casual clinging types that left a girl... breathless. He looked fresh and fabulous, and Amber's heart skipped and skittered in her chest.

"I missed him, too." She stroked Niko's velvet ears and gazed lovingly at his happy doggy face, crooning quietly. "Did you get the travel itinerary? Four days, four different states. Have you got someone to look after Niko?"

"My mum. She adores him." It was like her office had developed lungs and sucked the oxygen from the air. Amber felt dizzy, and she held onto Niko's soft, warm doggy body like she might a fine latte. Nate looked amazing.

"So, Niko will be at your mum's for the final two dates?" She wasn't sure she wanted the outcome of her show to be dictated by the persuasions of a dog. "You'd better warn the girls you come with a canine. I don't want them walking off set when they discover they have to share you with a dog." Niko rested his head in her lap, and she had to admit he was smart. A man's best friend? Or a friend's best man. Now that was a thought. She could use that idea… the camera panning to a lone man and his dog silhouetted against a rose-coloured sky. On a hill? A woman approaching in a flowing dress, the breeze gently lifting her hair. Hmmm. Sunset or sunrise?

"Are you still with us, Am?" Nate interrupted.

"I was just thinking of the finale. We should include Niko in the final screenshots. What do you think, mate? You could be a TV star." Niko banged his tail on the floor in response and they all laughed. Amber couldn't hide the pleasure she felt whenever Nate was near. Even more so since their date, but there was a sadness, too. She sighed and stroked Niko's head, and his liquid eyes looked up at her lovingly. Nate chuckled.

"You've won his heart, Am." His voice was husky, and she lifted her gaze to the blue study of his, his smile curling her toes. She loved him. The thought struck her like a beam of sunlight off clean glass. Of course, she did. Hadn't she told him love was forever? Love and hate were flipsides of the same coin. She loved him. She hated him. She loved him. For always, whether she wanted to or not.

"What time is your grammy's funeral on Friday?"

"One o'clock," she replied. "Cassie will oversee your date with Rebecca, and I'll catch up when I can."

He turned his attention to Cassie. "Is there any chance we can schedule the filming around the funeral? I think we should be there for Am… as friends." He directed his attention back to her. "You'll need support, and we'll be in Launceston anyway. I'm sure Rebecca would understand. You have a way about you, Am. The girls really like you."

"I think we could manage it," Cassie said slowly, her attention on the schedule in front of her. "What would we need? Three hours? Maybe four."

"That would be... nice, lovely, but really not necessary," Amber stammered. "Although there'll be country fare afterwards. Sponge cake, homemade sausage rolls, scones, lamingtons, and cups of tea."

"There's no way I'm missing out on your mum's scones." Nate grinned.

It seemed kind of fitting that Nate would be there to farewell her gram. Grammy was the only person who'd known how much Amber loved him, and how much of herself she'd lost when he'd publicly humiliated her. She fully planned to bury those feelings along with her gram. The thought tore at her heart, and she stifled the wave of emotion. Her gram was gone and the truth of it hadn't fully hit her yet. She'd been so busy, so distracted, but the funeral would be confronting.

"Okay," Cassie agreed. "I'll speak to Rebecca. I'm sure we can reschedule some of the activities she has planned to earlier in the day. No one in television land will know if we film lunch at eleven o'clock in the morning."

"Great. I've just spoken with John about product placement during the home visits. He's going to speak with you both shortly. I thought I'd pop in and give you a heads-up, but I'm more than happy with what we've come up with. Hopefully, you will be, too."

"I'm sure I will." Amber smiled. "We'll see you at the airport later. Tomorrow we'll drive out to Australia Zoo for the home visit with Nina. Are you feeling confident about meeting her family?"

"I'm sure they'll grill me, but if she were my daughter and the situation was reversed, I'd give me a hard time, too. It won't be easy for them knowing there are three other women sharing equally personal dates with me and that the awkwardness of the evening will be captured on national television."

"That's what leads to amazing footage," Amber said with satisfaction. "You're very brave. I'd be terrified."

"I am terrified, but I made a promise to someone who's important to me." He grinned. "For that person, I'd do whatever it takes to make up for the past, even if it means facing four furious families on their home turf." Nate called Niko and it was only after the pair of them reached the doorway and turned that he added with a bone-melting smile, "And hopefully earn her forgiveness."

Amber had assumed he was talking about Dan. He owed Dan his life. Of course, he would do whatever it took to repay him. *Her* forgiveness? He was doing this to make it up to *her*? What a cruel twist of fate. Somewhere in the heavens, the gods were laughing at her expense. A comedic tragedy unfolding on the stage of life. As a film producer, she appreciated the irony.

"Your expression just now was priceless." Cassie laughed. "I think every emotion got a look-in."

"That man will be the death of me." Amber moaned and took an oversized swig of her latte, nearly drowning in the caffeinated rush.

"You like him," Cassie surmised. "You *love* him? Still."

"No. Yes. No." Amber stood with a jerky movement. "Are we done here?"

"Not nearly. Sit. We have some important things to discuss."

"You're in cahoots with him, aren't you?" Amber sighed and lowered her weary bones into her seat. "This show is everything to me. It's more important than the fact that I might, might, still have feelings for a man who treated me badly. A long time ago. And I'd do well to remember that."

"Why are you holding onto age-old resentment? You know what that gets you…" Cassie stood. "Cancer and an early demise. Is that what you want? Or you could choose to forgive and forget and win the man."

"I want ratings success. I want *Bachelor on Board* to become a phenomenon, the first in a series of many. And I have my sights set on the first *Bachelorette on Board*. What do you think?"

"I think it's brilliant, but what about Nate? What about your feelings for him? Are you going to let the love of your life waltz off into the sunset with another woman?"

"It wouldn't be the first time." Amber's heart burned in her chest. "How does that saying go? Fool me once, shame on you. Fool me twice, shame on me? So yes, that's exactly what I'm going to do. I need him to waltz off into the sunset with the woman of his dreams on national television. And I need every woman in TV land to sigh and wish it was her."

"What if the woman of his choice is you?"

Amber's heart stilled. Her blood literally stopped in her veins and the shock momentarily stunned her. No. No. No. "That wouldn't work. That wouldn't work at all. Have you not been listening?"

"I've been watching. Watching when you think no one is looking. I see what you feel for him. I see how much it hurts you when he snuggles in close with one of the contestants."

"Teenage love is a beast. You don't just give your heart. You give your soul." Amber took a deep fortifying breath. "Forever. I gave him everything. I held nothing back when in truth it was utter fantasy. I'm a grown woman now, and I'm not going to fall for that delusion twice."

"Isn't that delusion what you're trying to sell to the television audience?" Cassie prodded. "If you don't believe in it, why should they? You've created romance in every scene. These women have fallen for Nate, for the fantasy, for the bewitchment that comes with love."

"I want that for them. I want that for Nate." Amber crushed the empty cup and threw it into the wastepaper basket. "I don't need it for me."

"I want that for you. I want that for me. You're just fighting it because loving Nate doesn't fit with your plans for the show. We can make it fit. I have an idea."

"There's no way I'm going to sabotage the success of this show." Tears of frustration welled in her eyes. She wasn't pining for him. She didn't need him. She didn't want him. There was not a chance she would entertain the idea of her and Nate and Niko as a family... frolicking with abandon on a pristine sandy beach. A mini-Nate sitting with his bucket and spade. A mini-Amber being thrown into the air with a squeal of delight. The waves splashing gently as Niko played in the shallows. Hell. The vision was as crystal clear as the trailer of a movie. Deluded. She dropped her eyes to the home visit schedule in front of her. Nate was as hapless as a fly in a web. Or maybe the fly was her, and the show was the big hungry spider.

"Amber, there's a way." Cassie's eyes lit up. "If you want it. There's a way we can work it into the show."

"Not without letting down four beautiful women who deserve better. I promised them a man. A husband. A prize."

"You know you're one of my best friends in the world, and I only want what's best for you. Do you need more coffee?"

"I don't like the sound of where you're going with this."

160

Amber squeezed her eyes closed and peered through her lashes at her overly animated friend. "And I don't like the look of it either."

"Don't you want to know how you can have both—a successful show *and* the man of your dreams."

"Nightmares, more like." But something unfurled in her chest and took root. A seed of hope.

"What if over the past couple of weeks, we've panned the cameras beyond the drama of the show to the reality in the wings?" Cassie gave her a moment to digest the unpalatable thought. "What if we've captured the way you two look at each other? Your interactions. What if we've captured the production meetings you have with Nate?" She looked hopeful. "Dates of a different kind… but maybe the audience will see that whilst romance is fanciful, love is real."

"Are you crazy?" Amber jumped to her feet, near knocking the schedules and itineraries to the floor. "You've done this? No, no, no. I can't do that to the girls. I'm not going to publicly humiliate them on national television and steal the prize. I can't do that."

"That does sound bad." Cassie nodded. "So, he goes through the motions, chooses a bride, proposes on national television and then when it's all over, he dumps her, and you step into the void?"

"No, no, no. That's worse. They've chosen their bridal gowns. They've visualised their dream wedding. The magazines have hounded them, and the world has seen the photos. He's perfect with these girls. No." She dropped back into her seat with resignation. "There's no way out of this."

"But you do love him," Cassie prompted.

"Yes." Damn, Cassie was good. She'd led her into that, and

Amber had fallen for it. Even without fresh coffee. "But I don't plan on acting on it. And I fully plan to bury the past along with Grammy and move on. My girls deserve their wedding. I promised them a prize. I'm not going to jeopardise that." She gathered her papers together. Nate wasn't good for her. She felt like a fool. A weak and spineless fool. It wasn't a feeling she liked. "Come on. We have a plane to catch."

"Really, Nate?" Amber observed the bottle of champagne in a bucket of ice, the flickering lights of tea candles in glass lanterns, and the fine glassware incongruently positioned on a picnic rug on the sand beside the surf. A picnic basket. Towels. Clearly, he'd bribed someone from the Twin Waters resort.

They'd all travelled to Maroochydore together and spent much of the flight planning the two episodes at Nate's home in Sydney.

Nate had suggested a walk along the beach before a late dinner, and Amber had agreed. They'd left their sandals and flip flops at the end of the concrete path leading from the resort to the surf and her feet were bare in the silky sand. Darkness had settled softly around them. "Is Cassie behind this?" She turned around, half expecting a film crew or a camera.

"I'm behind this. I want another date with you." His voice was quiet. He wore board shorts and a t-shirt and walked close enough beside her that his arm knocked against hers sending frissons of excitement through her body.

"Well, we can't. I've promised you to the contestants." She should have stepped away. She should have turned and run the moment she got wind of his plans. Instead, she stayed rooted to the spot and grappled for her breath. "How do you think they'll feel if they find out you're wining and dining the producer?

I can't do that to them, Nate. They're about to welcome you into their homes and introduce you to their families—become even more vulnerable in the eyes of the world. You have to find love with one of them."

"Love doesn't always play by the rules."

"We're not talking about love, and you know it. You don't believe in it, for one. For two, love comes with trust." She stopped. A week ago, she could have said she didn't trust him. But now? Hell. He wasn't the man she'd loved all those years ago. He was more. So much more.

"You expect me to trust those women? Trust has to be earned and you've had me on a pretty tight schedule. You must know how difficult it is to see through the fluff and nonsense to the real person behind the glamour and the makeup. Those women are blinded by television lights and deluded beyond sense by the crap they say to each other. I don't trust a single one of them. I trust *you*. Niko trusts you."

"Fine. You've made your point. The prenuptial agreement makes sense. You can raise it with them off screen, but I don't want the romance of your proposal ruined on screen."

"The romance of my proposal will be ruined by the fact that I'd rather be proposing to you."

He linked his fingers with hers and her brain, jammed. "Have you lost your mind?" The surf rolled and slapped against the sand, the sound like the crack of thunder. She tried to focus on the warm breeze—the way her sundress skimmed her bare legs. "You're crazy if you think I want that."

"I've seen the way you look at me, Am."

"You're wrong." She needed sunglasses as dark as the night. What if the contestants had seen it, too? Her show would be ruined.

"I feel the way you tense up when I'm near, the way the air snaps around us. You said you'd love me forever, and I've never stopped wanting you." His fingers gripped hers, and her fingers gripped his.

Stop it. That's not helping. She couldn't stop. His hand engulfed hers and the sensation brought stupid things to mind. Like safety and comfort and togetherness.

"That doesn't mean I want to act upon it. Or that I want to marry you." Damn it, she'd as good as said she loved him. Did she have no sense? What was it about Nathan Moretti that stripped her bare and left her exposed and vulnerable? She tore her eyes from his and stared at the white lace of the water as it frothed and churned and scurried away only to barrel towards the shore again.

"I want to marry you, and I know you won't believe me, but I love you, too."

She stopped and spun around to look at him, unable to believe her hearing. Had he really said the L word, or had she created it from that crazy part of her brain that thought this could somehow work out?

"I love you." He took both of her hands in his, and his gaze was earnest and raw with emotion.

Her vision became watery, and she couldn't wrestle her thoughts into order. "Nate, I forgive you for the past I do. There's no need to…"

"I'm not. This has nothing to do with the past and everything to do with now." He lifted her hands to his lips, and she fought the weakness that kept her eyes on his.

"You're deviating from the script and the script's important." Damn the tears. What was wrong with her? She was pathetic. Needy. Sad. Happy.

"I can't help how I feel."

He pulled her close and she melted into the heat of him, his scent filling her head with all kinds of delicious. When his lips sought hers, and his hungry tasting took her to heaven, she allowed herself to be swept away. Later, she'd realise she'd fallen for her own creation. Like a mad artist or a crazed scientist. The hours of editing, the careful angulation of the camera. His smile. The crinkles at the corners of his eyes. His laughter. His shadowed jaw. The way he looked at a woman as if she and only she could complete him. She'd fallen for an illusion of her own making.

But right now, she was so lost in the fantasy of Nathan Moretti she couldn't think. She brimmed with hope and desire and could scarcely draw breath. Here was magic. Here was what she wanted to feel. Special. Irresistible. Wanted. So wanted, a man would throw caution to the waves. So desired, he couldn't get close enough. So connected, a woman could lose sight of where she began, and he ended. He filled her head, and she could think of nothing else. She pressed against him, and he drew her close, so close she yearned—yearned for what she'd once traded her soul to taste. Worse, she needed him. She needed all that she'd denied she'd ever need again. Staying busy wasn't helping. Ignoring the pull of him wasn't working. He filled her heart, and she couldn't deny it any longer.

He scooped her into his arms, and she wrapped her legs around his waist. He stumbled towards the water, the warm embrace of it giving them privacy of a kind, and she laughed into the balmy night air as he dumped her unceremoniously into the waves. He found her again, drawing her wet and wild against him. She felt him, hard and full against her. Her body throbbed and ached. She wanted him. She wanted him more than the air she breathed. Their salty lips fell upon each other, and if she could have clambered closer, she would have. She tasted with abandon, and his hands traced her body to find her breasts. He took them with hands desperate to touch, to savour, to capture. Sensation roared, taking her from rapt to rapture. Here was what she'd longed for. Here was the only man who could complete her. The only man she'd ever loved. Here was her heart and her soul. Returned at last with every hungry groan. Here was Nate's heart given and received. The water swelled around them, and Nate took them deeper, lifting her to wrap her legs around him. She couldn't get close enough. There was only one place their frenetic coupling was headed, and Nate whispered his wishes aloud.

"Yes," she cried, and a gull screamed overhead.

"Thank God." His words were lost in the crash of the water, the breath of the wind. Nate's shorts were fought and won, the wisp of her underwear scarcely registering as it was pushed aside. He thrust deep inside her, his visceral groan melding with hers as she welcomed him with a small cry.

Don't stop, she thought as her body clung and raced and tore ahead of him, like the wind whipping the waves. The man in him held her close, even as the wolf in him pounced. She wrapped her legs tighter around his hips, drawing him closer then lifting herself away. His hands gripped the fleshy part of her buttocks and together they soared, higher than the waves, higher than the night sky above them, and when her climax rose and lifted her towards the heavens, he was with her, soothing and coaxing and pushing her onwards. Her elation was his as she surrendered to the sensations that sent her over the edge into bliss. Pure pleasure. Perfect union. She writhed and screamed and when the tempest passed, he knifed away and unleashed his control against her belly, pumping his seed into the swirling waves.

Amber collapsed against him, her head on his shoulder, her breath harsh and ragged against his neck.

Never had Nate been with a woman like this. Never had he made love with his whole heart. Amber bewitched and beguiled. As the sea surged around them, his legs barely kept them upright. He'd wanted to stay inside her forever, but his desire for release had stormed and raged. Never had he felt so perfectly attuned to a woman. Her scent nearly drove him to madness. Her mouth clung to his, and as he tasted and soothed and supped, his heart opened and filled and grew. Time ceased to exist. There was just Amber, finally where she belonged, in his arms, lithe and warm and wet—and insatiable.

Her kiss stoked a fire in his soul, and he slowly, slowly, slowly sank back into her heat. Deeper, closer, more urgent than before. Sensation roared in his ears, but he waited, fully sheathed. Still. Complete. Together. His arms encircled her, and he drew her closer, his kiss spinning a story of love. Of suffering and wanting and enduring. Her answer was one of gratitude and forgiveness and trust. Their pace was slow and steady and when her body tightened and pulsed, he leashed and fought the wolf until she was done, her cry touching him somewhere deep and primal, and when she collapsed against him, spent, he tore himself free and howled into the waves.

Holy smoke. The sea swirled around them, and he cupped his hand behind her head, his fingers tangling in her wet, siren-like hair, his mouth devouring and taking and giving.

"What have we done," she gasped, her mouth ripping from his. "What the hell have we done?"

"What we were destined to do." His tone soothed.

Her head dropped against his shoulder, and he felt the pounding of her heart against his chest. Strong. Determined. A force to be reckoned with. He lifted her chin with his hand and sought the fire in her eyes. "I love you. I want to marry you and somehow, we'll work this out."

"How, Nate, how?" Her words were anguished.

"Somehow." He straightened her clothing and straightened his own. "Let's find some food, and we'll work it out together. I'm not losing you again. Not ever." He took her hand in a grip that was tight enough to leave marks. His. She was his and no way would he lose her again. Not to the waves. Not to the night. Not to the twists of fate.

Amber huddled in a soft, fluffy towel, the comfort of its warmth way more than she deserved. What had she done? Oh my God. She glared at the night sky that sparkled and glittered beyond the water, the moon soft and benign. Traitor, she admonished herself. Fool. Love-sick, deluded fool.

She was flawed when it came to Nathan Moretti. She wanted to believe him. She wanted to believe in him, but this was madness, and it could cost her everything.

Somehow, she got through their dinner. So simple, so lovely, so special. Somehow, she made it back to her room. Somehow, she got through the next day. Seeing Nathan with Nina, meeting Nina's parents, smiling as if she meant it… ignoring the questions in Cassie's eyes. Ignoring the growl in Nate's.

Somehow, she got through his date with Rebecca, and survived the service, and here she stood by her grammy's graveside, in a black dress and black sunglasses, her heart torn and hurting. She watched as her grammy's coffin was lowered into the waiting space. There was the scent of the freshly turned earth, the shine of the sun on the brass fittings, and the scour of dirt as it slipped through her fingers and fell against the casket with a soft thud. Emotions threatened to choke her. The sky was blue and clear, and the birds trilled and called. Cassie stood respectfully, not far away. With Nate.

Grammy, you'd be ashamed of me. I'm ashamed of me. If you only knew—or perhaps you do know—how weak and sadly desperate I am. He says he loves me. He says he wants to marry me, but I'm scared. I'm a coward. I need you, Grammy. How will I cope without you?

Tears pooled and fell, and she blew her nose into a tissue that was well past its capacity to do the job. A fresh one appeared in her watery line of vision and she took it gratefully.

"You okay, Am?" Nate. His voice moved her like a perfectly pitched tone from a violin. His arm wrapped around her, and she sobbed, too weak to fight the feelings that overwhelmed her.

She was toast. She wanted him more than she had a right to want anyone, and she couldn't have him. She knew it. Deep down inside. Her grammy was wrong. Love couldn't conquer all. There were some situations that brought love to its knees. Like Rebecca, who'd spent the morning with Nate. Like Catherine who waited in Perth. Like Mia in Melbourne and Nina in Queensland. Like the television audience with their expectations of a happily-ever-after. On screen. On time. On schedule. With their favourite contestant.

The irony of it nearly choked her, but she took a deep breath, braced herself, and with a whispered farewell, turned away.

Worse, Ron waited in Sydney. Her mind shifted to their recent meeting. He'd been pleased, beyond pleased with the ratings, and he'd been more than positive about her ideas for *Bachelorette on Board*. Her career was a shooting star. She was headed for great things, but if she stole the prize from these girls? Her star would falter, peter out, and be gone. Worse, her show could go to… Jason? *Bachelor on Board* had trumped *The Amazing Race* in the ratings, and where she was discussing the option of more shows, he was done. She should be whoohoo'ing and happy dancing, not contemplating the worst career move known to man.

Worse, she'd be publicly humiliated and ridiculed in every newspaper and magazine. Every radio talk show. The drama of high school would be a poor cousin compared with the hate of a national television audience—bigger, way bigger, than she could have dreamed possible. She'd never work in the television industry again. Jason's self-satisfied smirk appeared in her mind's eye, and she forced it away, shifting her gaze to the beloved countryside around her. The cemetery overlooked the town, and as she walked quietly towards their black hire car, she heard the sound of cows lowing in the neighbouring paddocks.

She couldn't do it. She couldn't.

Nate beeped the lock release and Amber yanked the rear door open. The smell of new leather blasted her from the sun-heated interior. She lowered herself into the seat and Cassie got in from the opposite side. She squeezed Amber's hand, and Amber gave her a weak smile.

"It's gorgeous here, Am."

Amber nodded before leaning forward to give Nate directions to the football clubhouse where there would be tea and cake. His date that morning with Rebecca had gone well. He'd appeared casual and relaxed, but every stroke of his hand against Rebecca's face, every intimate word they'd shared had scored her like a blade. Perhaps with Grammy's funeral, she was more vulnerable than usual. The agony of being in the vicinity of Nate with another woman had been too much to bear.

She couldn't do this anymore.

She had to do this. She had to see it through. In Melbourne. In Perth. But how was she to hold it together? Tonight, Nate would be embraced by Rebecca's family and grilled with regards to his intentions. She would have to stand there, coax him through it, smile, make conversation, drink too much coffee knowing she'd lay awake half the night, knowing what she'd done, knowing what she wanted.

Nate.

And then there was the editing. Even if she survived the filming, she'd have to relive it over and over as she created the show.

The car bumped over the pot-holed road which led to the clubhouse, and she directed Nate to pull up on the grassy verge. She took a deep breath and tried to master the crazy inside her head. *You can do this. You'll be fine. One breath at a time.*

"Come on, Am," Cassie urged. "Let's go and celebrate your grammy's life and then we'll get you out of here."

Amber looked at her friend with gratitude. "I think after this, I might need some alone time," she whispered. "Do you think…?"

"I could oversee the filming at Rebecca's tonight? Absolutely."

"Thank you." Amber sighed with relief and turned her attention towards Nate, who'd come around to open her door. Damn, he was gorgeous. Her heart tripped, and her insides melted. His gaze captured hers.

"Are you okay?"

No, she wanted to say. No, I'm not okay. No, I'm not fine. It's not getting any better. The tears started afresh, and she grappled in her bag for another tissue.

"Here." He handed her one and together they walked towards the yellow brick building, their heels crunching on the gravel. The sun was warm on her back but all she could sense was Nate's blistering touch against her arm. She heard Cassie's voice from a distance, belying her closeness, and she fought to hide her feelings, so raw, so private. She needed to smile and greet people, make banal, useless conversation, and get through the next hour until she could return to the hotel and give in to the giant swell of tears inside of her.

She took a deep, grounding breath, and accepted the teacup thrust into her hands by her father, her gaze colliding with his. She wasn't the only one hurting, and she gave in to the need to hold him close. The cup rattled in her hand and Nate took it from her before she scalded herself. She sank into her father's embrace and held on.

"It's okay, sweetheart. You know it is."

"I'm fine, Dad," she mumbled against him, telling him what he wanted to hear. Hell, she was good at that. Lilydale was a part of her. Just like her grammy was. Her father was right. It would be okay. "Thank you."

"I love you, sweetheart," he comforted.

"I love you too, Dad."

Her father eased back and gazed into her face. "Have you had something to eat. Come on." He led her to the table and placed a plate in her hand. In Lilydale, there was no problem scones couldn't fix. She loaded hers with jam and cream, then reached for an extra plate and scone for Nate. She turned to find him there, waiting with her tea.

"Here." She smiled. "One of Mum's scones."

"You're the only woman for me." He took the plate and placed her tea on a tall circular table set up to mingle around.

"I should be helping out in the kitchen." The hum of people talking and greeting each other was more like a school picnic than a sombre occasion. She acknowledged people's condolences, accepted hugs, and smiled when she needed to. She managed to swallow half a scone before she gave up and reached for her tea.

Cassie joined them and exclaimed over the hearty country fare. Nate raved about his lamington and lifted a piece to Amber's mouth… She felt Cassie's sympathy and shifted her attention to the crowd of people. Many she'd known since she was a child. Her grammy was much loved by the entire community, and it seemed the entire township of Lilydale had come to say their farewells.

Amber got through the polite conversation, the gentle support, and the camaraderie of a township where everyone knew everyone. It was what she loved and hated about Lilydale in equal measure. If Cassie hadn't accompanied her and Nate, there would have been questions in the weathered brows of her family's neighbours, but no, she appeared prim and proper as a bereaved granddaughter should. No need for hushed whispers yet… the thought was an anathema. What was she to do?

Chapter Eleven

Please come and see me. The moment you're free.

Ron wanted to see her? Amber fought the urge to pick up her laptop and hurl it across the small café where she sat, not far from her company's office in McMahons Point. She'd survived the Perth and Melbourne home visits and managed to avoid any alone time with Nate for the past two days. The final key ceremony was to be filmed on the superyacht that evening, before the final two home visits with Nate's family in Coogee in Sydney. The final four girls had returned to the boat, and Nate was no doubt back in his bachelor pad on the top deck.

Amber reached for her coffee and took a gulp. There was another *urgent* email, this time from her cinematographer. "Amber, please check out this footage and work out what you'd like to do with it."

On impulse she clicked the link.

Okay, so she'd check it out, then meet with Ron, then get back on set. Every cell in her body resisted it. The effort required to maintain her professional facade was exhausting, but there was no way out. She just had to focus on the filming and be objective. Pretend. Go through the motions like her heart hadn't been gored, like her brain wasn't seared with memories of Nate's touch.

The movie played out silently on the screen in front of her, and her coffee went cold as she sat transfixed. How had she not known the camera was on her? How had she been so oblivious? The camera panned on her and Nate and Niko on the beach. Her feelings for Nate were clear on her face. The chemistry between them practically sizzled. Shots of her directing the cameras, her attention drawn to Nate. Attraction. Pain. Love? The beach at Cape Leveque... the sunset. The fire. They'd filmed it? From where? She'd thought she and Nate were alone. Her privacy had been invaded and anger licked at her like flames.

What of their picnic at Twin Waters? Had someone filmed that, too? Oh, hell. Guilt tore at her gut. It had been dark. The waves had given them privacy, but what of the moonlight? Had someone seen them? Her breath caught sharply in her windpipe. No. There was footage of their walk along the beach. So close. So intimate. Their kiss. Their laughter. Then the funeral. Perth. Melbourne. There was footage going back weeks. Nate's feelings were there, too. His care and attention. She saw what she hadn't noticed until that moment. He watched her, too. His gaze followed her across the set. His brow furrowed when he thought he was alone.

Amber sat like stone.

So, he loved her, and she loved him. The footage told a story more real, more moving, more gut-stirring than the staged dates she'd so carefully edited. Hope surged for the shortest moment like a shooting star in the night sky before she snuffed it out. This didn't change anything. Sure, she could intersperse it with the other dates to win the audience over. To help them see what had brewed between her and Nate off set. Perhaps they'd forgive her, perhaps they'd even want them to get together—somehow—but it didn't change her promise to the contestants. The women who had put their hearts on the line. On national television.

Without them, she wouldn't have a show. She knew exactly how they'd feel if she added this footage. Humiliated. Foolish. All four of them had confessed to having feelings for Nate. Both Mia and Catherine had used the L word. To say *I love you* on national television and to feel set up? She couldn't do it. She liked these women too much. She wanted them to find love. But with Nate?

Damn it, she loved him, too.

She wanted to scream with frustration. She'd fought her feelings for Nate. He was a far cry from the teenager she'd loved. He'd grown into a man she respected. He was caring and genuine and considerate. Nate had told her he loved her and wanted to marry her, but it was like a mirage. Real yet false. Right there yet impossible to grasp. It hurt. So much. And she loved Niko. Tears welled, and her heart felt twisted and tangled in her chest. Hell. She had to go and face Ron. Game-face on Amber, she lectured herself. You can do this. Remember what's important.

She closed the link and pushed her laptop into her bag.

With a last disgusting swig of her now cold coffee, she swung her bag over her shoulder and walked the short distance along Victoria Street towards the executive offices. What could Ron possibly want? She needed to get back and get sorted for tonight's ceremony. She needed to speak with the girls. And tell them what?

Amber sat in the small reception area and waited to be called through. Ron's secretary gave her a sympathetic smile. The executive offices were formal and hushed like a library. Wood panelling and glossy surfaces reflected her too-pale face as she was waved in.

"Hi, Ron." Amber's professionalism was too ingrained to allow her inner turmoil to show. She took his proffered hand and lowered herself into the dark leather chair opposite him. Ron observed her over his desk and was silent for a long moment. Her pulse leapt in her throat, which was ridiculous because the last time she'd seen him, he'd been full of glowing praise. The ratings were exceptional. He'd embraced her ideas for future shows. There was no reason for the unease that slipped along her shoulder blades. She straightened the fabric of her skirt and clenched her toes in her high-heeled shoes, forcing herself to release them and relax.

"Thanks for coming in, Amber. I know you're busy."

"That's okay. What's up?" Fear gripped her by the throat.

"I had Jason in here this morning, and he tells me we have a problem with the finale."

"We do?" Amber's pulse went from leaping to hammering. What the hell had Jason done? Was there no end to his jealous sniping?

"He tells me your bachelor's unlikely to fall for any of the contestants." Ron leaned back in his leather desk chair and clasped his hands, making a steeple with his fingers under his chin. He studied her, his gaze steady.

"How would he know that?" She clamped down on the whimper of panic that bubbled in her throat. *You can do this. You'll be fine.*

"He tells me your bachelor has fallen for you." His brow lifted, and his gaze burned into her like a laser. She squirmed under his scrutiny, her heart a percussive staccato, her head dizzy with the spin of her thoughts.

Crap, crap, crap. How could Jason know that, and why would he tell Ron? Because he wanted her to fail. Her ratings had outshone his. He had to pull her down. How had she ever found him attractive?

"Nate signed a contract and promised to propose to one of the contestants. He's looking for a wife, and he will find one. On the show. We've just filmed the home visits and all four of the women admitted they have feelings for him. Two said they loved him."

"What about you?" Ron asked, his tone gentle. "How do you feel about Nate? I understand there's a history between you."

"We went to high school together, and we dated a long time ago. Not ideal, but when Dan and Christina left the show, I didn't have much choice, and Nate was a good Plan B."

His gaze held hers, his brow creased. "So, you *do* have a history?"

"Yes, but it shouldn't be a problem." How the hell had Jason discovered that? He was a journalist. No doubt he had his insidious ways. "We're good… friends." Friends? When she thought back over the past several weeks, yes, they were definitely that. That's what they were. Friends. With benefits? She flushed as the old cliché came to mind, her cheeks warming as she studied the polished timber of Ron's desk. Hell.

"Amber?"

"Yes?"

"You know the media will keep tabs on Nate after the show. If he goes through the motions of proposing for the sake of the contract and then dumps the winning contestant after the cameras stop rolling to hook up with the producer…the next series will flop."

She'd already thought of that. "Yes. I agree."

"So how are you going to manage this?"

"I have a few ideas," she blundered, feeling the universe tip and her feet lose traction.

"Would any of them involve Nate falling in love and proposing to a contestant?" His gaze bored into hers.

"This is a reality show, Ron. I've done everything in my power to create romance and the perfect setting for love, but real life is complicated. Love doesn't always happen by the script, on time and as scheduled, despite my best efforts."

"It's your job to ensure Nate proposes to the woman he loves." He paused. "Have I made myself clear?"

"Yes, sir." Her head throbbed.

"The public have embraced your bachelor. You've captured something in their imagination. What you've done so far is brilliant. You're an outstanding, creative producer. Find a way to fix this."

Amber nodded. She couldn't speak. Her throat hurt. Her head pounded. Her heart wept.

"It's important to be honest with yourself and your audience."

A frown creased her brow. What exactly was Ron suggesting? "Okay." She rose to her feet and straightened her skirt. "I'll do my best."

"I know you will. You're good at what you do, Amber. Find a way to give your audience a satisfying ending."

"I will." She clutched the strap of her bag and turned to leave. She had to speak to Nate. He appeared deeply involved with each of the women, which was great for television, but hell on earth for the woman who loved him.

"Amber?"

"Yes, sir?" She turned in the doorway.

"You look exhausted. I was sorry to hear about your grandma."

"Thanks, Ron." Emotion rose in her throat. She had to leave before she dissolved into a puddle on the floor. "And thanks for the flowers."

Mia and Catherine.

The two women stood with their keys as Nina and Rebecca shared dismayed glances. The key ceremony had taken most of the night to film, and Amber felt sick with fatigue. She was tired of watching beautiful women smooch with Nathan in nothing but bikinis... of trying not to look at his bare chest in the jacuzzi... of trying to do the right thing. The television audience didn't want authenticity. They wanted the fantasy, the sniping, the alcohol-fuelled rants, the party. Did they really want Nate to find love? That was the key question. If yes, then they wouldn't care whether he found love with a contestant... or the producer. The footage she'd studied could be drip-fed into the second half of the show so that by the final scene, they would welcome Nate's proposal—proposal? Was she willing to go that far? To sign a prenuptial agreement—she didn't care about his money—and marry him? Neanderthal Nathan?

Hell. It was the only word she had time to think before she was catapulted to the ground by a heavy weight from behind her, and the set became bedlam.

"Niko!" she heard Nate call. "Niko!"

How had Niko ended up on set? He ran amok amongst the cables and the girls. He leapt against their dresses and shot through the crowd like a runaway thief as Nate tried to catch him. The girls screamed and Niko barked with excitement.

Amber took a moment to get back on her feet. "Niko!" She and Nate lunged after his wily body and ended up in a chaotic pile of limbs and dog. She couldn't stop the laughter. It bubbled up and with Nate's arms around her, she was lost in the magic of his embrace. His tux felt superbly smooth, his scent like a breath of heaven. Her body stirred, low and deep, pounding like the stroke of midnight.

Nate pulled Niko's weight off her and she struggled to right herself. Her gaze drifted to Nate's and he winked, sending her heart into freefall.

Neither Mia nor Catherine appeared enamoured by Nate's best mate. Mia was in tears because he'd ripped her dress, and Catherine had settled with her on the couch. "Where the hell did the dog come from?" she demanded, her tone furious.

Nina and Rebecca's farewells had been filmed before Niko's fall from grace, but between the girls, the crew, and the equipment, the scene was chaotic.

"Nate, I'll take Niko back upstairs. Can you fix things here?" Amber reached for Niko's collar, and he looked up at her with pure love and happy fizz, his tongue taking a swipe at her, completely oblivious to the damage he'd caused. "Look what you've done," she scolded in a whisper, "You've made the lovely Mia cry."

Or maybe Mia had burst into tears because she was beyond tired. There was nothing easy about filming this show, and it was unscripted, which left a lot to chance. And chance had been kind so far. She wasn't sure a dog pawing the women's long gowns was remotely fair, but it had created some excitement in an otherwise falsely dramatic scene. Nina was the only one who'd stayed calm, the rest were like hysterical children.

Amber risked a final glance and saw that Nate had worked

his magic. What was it about him? He seemed to know just what to say to soothe and smooth. Like a sixth sense. He had an innate charisma, and she felt sorry for herself as she led the recalcitrant mutt back up to the top deck. How odd. The lock was usually engaged, and Nate had been on the set the whole night. Perhaps the latch hadn't closed properly? But Niko could hardly have pulled the door towards him.

She knelt and stroked Niko's velvet ears. No doubt he was sick of being alone, and she couldn't blame him. She knew just how he felt. Truly? Was she ready to share her life? Did she really want to reach out and make this happen? She could. The possibility prickled her skin. She could do this. She could work it into the script so the public would want her and Nate to get together. The footage her cinematographer had taken was good. Inspired. The footage with Niko might be helpful, too. She smiled down at him. Neither Mia nor Catherine had reacted well to Niko. Niko was a big part of Nate's life. Perhaps neither one of them was the right woman for Nate after all and once the glitter and shine of the television fantasy was gone, the relationship would fail. She stroked Niko, and he snuggled his head into her lap.

"I have to get back," she whispered and gazed into his adoring eyes. "You behave while I'm gone." Clapping sounded from behind her, and she twisted sharply.

"Oh, how heart-warming. Where are the cameras when you need them?"

Jason. "What are you doing here lurking in the darkness? Trespassing. Don't you have a show to run? A race to finish?"

"Funny you should ask about that. The final edits are done, and I find myself at a loss now that the show has been cut."

"Oh, I'm sorry to hear that." Amber rose, her hand on Niko's collar. The dog growled and pulled against her hold. There was something in Jason's tone Niko didn't like. She didn't much like it herself. "So why are you here?"

"I was in the area, and I wanted to talk to you. I saw the lights on."

"I suppose it was you who let Niko through to where we were filming." Of course, it was, she thought to herself. He'd tried to sabotage her filming yet again. Was there no end to his malice? "What was so urgent that you needed to find me at four in the morning?" She smelled alcohol on his breath, and her gaze shifted to his dishevelled clothing. The light from the quay lengthened the night shadows and eerily punctuated the twisted emotion on Jason's face.

"I want you back, babe. I made a mistake. I was a fool. We had something good going, didn't we?"

"The emphasis being on the past tense." Amber tightened her grip on Niko's collar. "We did have something good, but you threw it away when you treated me like a steppingstone."

"Oh, come on, babe." His words were slurred. "You have brilliant ideas all the time. It was no biggie to share one with me."

"You set me up, you snake in the grass. You never loved me, and I won't settle for anything less."

"You haven't truly fallen for your bachelor, have you? That bloke downstairs is a figment of your imagination. He doesn't exist. You've created a man your audience will fall in love with, but he's fictional, my darling. He's not real. I am."

"You thought you'd share that with Ron, didn't you? And try to undermine the success of my show. That's despicable."

"I may have mentioned something, but only out of concern for you. I didn't want your show to bomb, and Nathan as good as agreed he'd fallen for you. Don't sabotage the success of your show for him. I love you way more than he ever could."

"I doubt that somehow." The dulcet tones of her lead man cut into the conversation. He stood framed in the doorway to the stairs, a long-stemmed rose in his hand. "I believe you're on private property."

"Well, it's hardly yours mate, or perhaps you've fallen for this fiction as well? I hate to break it to you, but you're an employee, and Amber here is your boss."

"You know the appeal of an office romance, Jason, but unless I'm mistaken, the lady isn't interested. It's time to move on or I'll call security."

Niko pulled on his collar with a low-pitched growl, and Amber struggled to hold him back.

Jason's reactions were slow and sluggish, but he lifted his hands defensively. "Nice dog." Niko bared his teeth.

"If you don't go right now, I'm going to let this nice dog loose," she threatened. "He sounds like he'd like to play, or maybe that's not what he has in mind."

"You've changed, Amber, and not in a good way." Jason's gaze assessed the animosity in Niko's. "I'm not done."

"But I am Jason. Now leave."

Jason's attention flicked towards Amber before returning to Niko. "I'll see myself out."

"You do that. You have until I count to five." She waited. "One. Two."

Jason lurched away. He banged the elevator button and looked relieved when the doors opened.

"Good riddance." Nate grinned.

Amber released Niko and he took off like a crazy critter towards the elevator door, barking nonstop.

Nate extended the rose towards Amber and with a smouldering look in his eye said, "Amber, will you accept this rose?"

She practically wept when his gaze captured hers, and she saw what shone there. Love. For her. She took the thornless stem, the sweet scent of it swirling between them. "Thank you." He took her into his arms, and she was too tired to fight the syrupy desire in her veins. "Two more dates, then the finale." Her words vibrated against his chest.

"You're the only woman I want to propose to, Am." Nate pushed her back and gazed into her eyes. "No way is Niko going to choose Mia or Catherine."

"They hardly had a chance. He bounded out of nowhere."

"First impressions. He did that to you, too, and you passed the test."

"I didn't know it was a test and neither did they. Let's wait and see how the home visits go. When they realise, he's *your* dog, their feelings towards Niko will change."

"Then their feelings towards Niko will be false. As false as their feelings towards me."

"They both said they love you, on screen, in front of millions of viewers. If that isn't real, I don't know what is."

"This is." Nate cupped her face with both hands and lowered his mouth to hers. His kiss spoke of many things and the messages spun in Amber's exhausted brain. Tender. Yes. He tasted with a raw emotion that told her he cared. Her response was equally heated, and then there was just the two of them. Every stroke of his tongue, every sweet sensation was like a symphony, swelling with a thousand notes.

The staccato of her pulse roared in her ears, and she gave in to the pull of his body, pressing against him like a shameless hussy. He wanted her. She wanted him, and as much as she wanted the show to succeed, she wanted him more.

"I love you." He drew back the minutest fraction to gift the words against her lips. "I love you." His kisses blazed along her jaw to her ear. "I love you." The words sizzled against her neck.

"I love you, too," she groaned, the words torn from a part of her that had never healed. A part of her that was his and his alone. A part so primal, so enduring that she couldn't live without him.

"I know." He nuzzled closer and sent her body into freefall. "I'm not whole without you. I need you. Even before I knew it, I needed you."

"I need you, too." Her joy was so sharp it hurt.

"I want you more than I can say." His kisses burned against her skin. "I'll never stop wanting you."

"I want you, too. More than I should." Desire roared through her veins.

"Say you'll marry me." His lips hovered against hers, urgent and hungry.

"I'll think about it." Her eyes sought his. "And it's not about the prenup. I'm happy to sign that. I don't care about your millions." Her words were lost as he tasted, supped, devoured. She devoured right back… and later, she discovered the whole moment had been captured by her chief cinematographer. The man was sneaky. Sneaky but smart because it was a moment worth catching. An intimate, precious moment too soon lost as Nate scooped her into his arms and carried her off to his bachelor lair. Beyond the cameras. Beyond the public eye to a place where there was only Nate and Amber, and what raged between them.

Chapter 12

Coogee was a hip, bustling, beachside metropolis. Amber had fought the rigidity in her bones as Nate and Mia walked together along the Bondi to Coogee Coastal Walk, lounged in ocean pools cut into the headlands, and chatted over an intimate lunch at a beachside bar.

Now, she battled a gazillion butterflies as they made their way along the footpath to Nate's mum's house, a stunning, contemporary home perched on a ridge overlooking Gordon's Bay. It was late afternoon, but the sun was still warm, and the sky was a cloudless blue.

Nate appeared enamoured with Mia—smitten—and doubt dug its spurs into Amber's heart. What if he changed his mind at the last minute, and she was humiliated on national television? How could she trust Neanderthal Nathan not to be playing her? She would never be able to show her face again. She'd have to have surgery and change her identity. She'd have to move to Bali or India or Pakistan.

Mia looked up at him, her eyes shining, and pulled him close. Amber's heart nearly stalled in her chest. This was insane. She didn't have the grit for this. She was on tenterhooks, and how had she allowed herself to become a contestant on her own show?

Mia wore stilettos and a beautiful white dress, her blonde hair cascading down her back in a silken wave. She was tanned—the real thing—her body toned and slender, and she carried a huge bouquet of flowers for Nate's mum.

Cassie reached over and pulled Amber close. "Mia's nervous, too. I can hear it in her breath."

"She's incredible. What was I thinking?" Amber's voice was a strangled whisper. This process was excruciating, and the closer they got to the finale, the more her skin itched with a bad case of hives. "I can't compete with her."

The front door opened, and Niko came bounding through, dashing first to Nate, his tail wagging like a whip, and then to Mia, who screamed and dropped her flowers to the ground. Niko licked at her hand, but she snatched it back, her body rigid. Niko bounced away and headed in a mad rush towards Amber. She grabbed for his diamond-studded collar.

"Niko." He deserved a scolding, but he gave her that familiar doggy-grin, and her insides softened to mush. She settled herself on her knees to give him a cuddle, grateful for the jeans, tee, and converse runners she'd decided to wear. She was working. She wasn't here to impress Nate or his mum or his sister. She was here to make this episode the best it could be. Niko leaned into her, and she couldn't stop the laugh when he tried to lick her.

"I'm sorry, Nate!" A slim girl dressed all in black—tight jeans, ripped top, and combat boots—with a studded choker, dark lipstick and heavy eye make-up ran towards him, clinging to him like he was a soldier returned from active duty. "I've missed you so much. I'm glad you're home. Finally!"

"Mia, this is Bella, my younger sister. Bella, this is Mia. And that was Niko, my dog, who is still learning his manners." Bella grinned at Mia, before she dived past to help Amber with Niko. Mia picked up the flowers and fought for a smile. To her credit, she pulled herself together, and Nate drew her towards the doorway, where his mum waited with quiet dignity. "And this is my mum, Beverley." Mia greeted her with a warm smile and gifted her the flowers.

Amber waited while the camera crew followed Nate inside. "You must be Bella. I'm Amber." Bella had a number of piercings through her nose and lip. Her long hair was ombre-coloured, moving from black to blonde to pink. Minus the Goth trimmings, she was beautiful.

"Nate told me you dressed like me at school."

"I didn't want to conform to the school's idea of beautiful." She couldn't compete for starters, and perhaps she'd wanted to show how little she cared about anyone else's opinion.

"Exactly." The younger woman tossed her hair back with a grin. "And I don't want to look anything like my stepmother."

"Yeah, Nate told me about her."

"I wish I'd met you during your Goth phase. Nate told me how beautiful he thought you looked. But then he took that stupid Bethany to the formal. Men don't think with their brains."

Amber was speechless. Had Bella just implied she dressed like that because of her? And Nate had thought she looked beautiful back then? Her thoughts left her in a spin, and she floated through the motions of handing over Niko, catching up with Cassie, and directing the proceedings. The house was spectacular with floor to ceiling windows and terraces that opened up to a wide expanse of sea, sky, and beachside vegetation.

The dinner conversation flowed along with the wine, and

Mia fitted in perfectly with the expensive lux of the house. She got along well with Beverley, who was kind and welcoming, but Bella seemed more rebellious and unwilling to warm towards her.

It was towards the end of the shoot, as Amber leaned against the bench in the modern, stylish kitchen, that Beverley came up behind her.

"Mia's a charming girl."

"Yes, she is, and I think Nate genuinely likes her." Amber was exhausted from battling her doubts and her fears—maybe he'd told Mia he loved her and wanted to marry her, too—and she was close to tears with worrying that Nate might change his mind.

"But I know my son, and I've seen the way he looks at you. The way you look at him."

Amber's chest tightened and adrenalin shot through her veins faster than the caffeine she'd craved. "Yes, well, our friendship is kind of complex."

"I imagine it must be." Beverley stood beside her, and together they watched Nate and Mia in silhouette against the rosy sky. "You broke his heart once before you know, and I'm really not keen to see him hurt again."

From where she was standing, his heart looked just fine, pumping as it was in the arms of another woman. It was *her* heart that felt like it had been crushed to a pulp and couldn't fathom a beat. "I'm surprised to hear that. He moved on pretty quickly back then."

"Looks can be deceiving." Her gaze shifted back to Amber.

"Yes, but sometimes where there's smoke, there's fire." Her tone was petulant, and she took a swig of her coffee.

"Nate told me about your grammy. I'm sorry for your loss."

"Thank you." Tears welled in her eyes, and she swiped them away. Nate's mum reached over and pulled her into a hug. She smelled sweet, her perfume subtle and scarcely there, her embrace, squishy and warm.

"Thank you for supporting Bella's cause. It's really important to us, and I'm guessing you're behind the network's proposed documentary about the clinic and the business?"

"The idea of troubled teens working to keep their clinic open after their funding was cut will capture the community's attention and help to build awareness around adolescent mental health issues, which are so prevalent. Hopefully, we'll encourage the government to prioritise funding. Television is a powerful medium."

"I've been watching the show, and I have to say I'm impressed with how you've shown the women behind the faces, and the man behind the money."

"Love and family were a big part of my childhood, but money wasn't. If I hadn't won a scholarship to Sydney Grammar, my life would have been very different."

"Yes, money is important. Bella was lucky we could afford the care she needed. Many teenagers in less privileged circumstances turn to drugs."

"Yes." Amber drained her cup and lowered it into the sink. "And that's what the clinic does for these teenagers. It gives them a sense of self-respect and belonging. I want the government to recognise the importance of that, and the lives that it saves. Bella was lucky to have you and Nate."

"Nate knows the importance of family, better than most."

"Yes." Amber smiled at the older woman. Beverley wore a soft grey cashmere top over black pants, and looked very stylish, but she was quietly confident and humble. There was a warmth to their home despite the reams of glass, and Amber really admired Nate's mum. She didn't miss much either. "I think we're ready to wrap this up, and you can get back to your evening."

Bondi Beach in early November was busy, and the day had turned out to be a beauty. Catherine and Nate were in the surf, and their laughter carried across the waves. Nate was giving her a surfing lesson, and Amber had to admit the iconic beach made for some great footage, along with their wet, limber bodies. Amber stood in shorts and a tee on the shore, directing the footage.

As Nate and Catherine collapsed onto their towels on the sand, Amber saw a woman approach in a scarcely-there red bikini, her hair a smooth bottle-blonde.

"I'd be careful with this one, honey. He doesn't want a family. You'll find it hidden somewhere in the fine print of the prenuptial agreement he'll get you to sign before he'll even propose to you, let alone marry you. Don't be fooled."

"Cut the cameras." Nate demanded. "What are you doing here, Megan."

"Done." Amber's voice was weak. He didn't want children? He didn't want a family? How could she not have asked him about that?

"I'm his stepmother, honey. And I know him pretty well." The blonde woman dropped her sunglasses back on her nose.

Amber stood frozen, the drama unfolding before her like a slow-moving tsunami.

"I don't know too many young women who don't want a child of their own one day. Or many who like the idea of being left high and dry financially if their husband leaves. Your

Bachelor there has a wandering eye. How many women is he playing you off against? From what I hear, it's more than one. You might want to ask him about that."

Nate stood rigid, his expression one of pure hatred. "Sour grapes, Megan. You have no right to interfere."

"Just protecting what's mine, Nathan. And last I checked, we're on a public beach." She turned her attention back to Catherine, who looked confused. "Don't be fooled, honey. Ask him about the prenup." She nodded towards Amber. "And ask him about her."

Amber's stomach churned and pulled, and she nearly lost her breakfast. This couldn't be happening. Megan adjusted her itsy-bitsy bikini top, which scarcely covered her very generous breasts and sauntered off, a satisfied smile on her face.

Catherine turned to Nate with a confused expression. "What was she talking about? What prenuptial agreement? And why do I need to ask about Amber?" Catherine knelt to shove her things into her bag. "When were you planning on filling me in?

"A prenuptial agreement doesn't make my feelings any less real, and it doesn't mean you'll be left high and dry financially."

"So, it's true. If I win, you expect me to sign a prenup? A prenup that stipulates you don't want children?"

"Financially, it's a generous arrangement, and the longer the marriage lasts, the greater the percentage of my fortune you'd be entitled to. We haven't known each other very long, but I am attracted to you and I do like you a lot." He swept a wet lock of hair away from his eyes. "I'd really like you to meet my mum and I'd really like a chance to explain.' He paused, his gaze on the water. 'I come from a broken home, and I never want to put a child through what my parents put my sister and me through."

Amber's legs buckled. This was beyond unendurable. The prenup stipulated no children? How could she sign away the family she'd always wanted? *Oh, Grammy.*

"You never want to have children?" Catherine's voice had a slight hysteria to it, and Amber felt an ache in the region of her ovaries.

"No."

His stepmother knew how to pack a punch. Catherine was left reeling. Amber was left reeling. *Bachelor on Board* was a farce. What the hell did this mean for the finale?

The home visit with Catherine was less than a frivolous affair. Beverley, bless her, kept it together, but when she tried to catch Amber's eye, Amber looked away. The tape would need serious editing, but hopefully she could pull it together. Catherine stood alone on the terrace outside, her gaze on the darkening sky, and Beverley took Nate aside.

Amber would have to speak with her, but she didn't know what to say. Nate had calmed the situation, and whatever he'd said to Catherine had smoothed things over enough for the home visit to go ahead. She'd rightly been Nate's first priority, but Amber felt excluded and snarky.

When had he planned to tell *her* about the fine print in the prenup?

Neanderthal Nathan, it seemed, was the same old wolf in sheep's clothing. How had she been stupid enough to fall for it twice? She stormed around the living area, unable to sit, oblivious to Cassie's worried gaze, and Bella's questioning one.

Niko stayed on her heels, his wet nose occasionally bumping

against her bare legs.

Amber gave up. She threw the mic and head piece to Cassie and took herself out into the street. She couldn't bear another moment. It was bad enough that she had to worry about whether he'd fallen for another woman, but now she had to accept that if she wanted Nate, she would never have a family. She sat on the curb, her head in her hands, and fought to control her breath.

Someone settled themselves beside her and stroked her back. "Amber, are you okay?" It was Bella, and the tears that had threatened all afternoon found their way to the surface.

"I'm fine," she lied. "Really. It's okay. Thanks."

"You love him, don't you?" Her tone was gentle, like she was soothing a baby, which was an irony since Amber was crying for the babies she could never have—with Nate.

"Yes, but it's not that simple." Amber fought to catch her breath.

"When my parents went through their divorce, I thought it was my fault." Bella's tone was soft.

"After meeting your stepmother today, I very much doubt that. Is that why you wear black? Because you're in mourning?"

"How did you know?"

"Because I know how important my dad is to me, and you must feel like you lost yours when he left, but I'm sure he loves you." What had Nate said? He didn't want to have children because he didn't want any child to suffer the way he and his sister had suffered.

"My dad is incapable of loving anyone but himself, but I'm okay with it. And my mum is happier without him. I'm happier without him, too."

"I'm sorry you've been through such a terrible time."

"It made me stronger, but I think Nate is very confused about marriage."

"Oh, you do, do you?" Nate's voice sounded from behind them, a smooth, dulcet tone that plucked Amber's insides like strings. She was past help. Past sanity. Past knowing what she should do.

"Can I speak with Amber please? Alone."

Bella got to her feet. "If you mess this up, I'll never forgive you." She stormed away leaving a lingering blast of spicy sweet perfume.

"Confused about marriage is one way to put it." Amber tried to keep the cynicism from her voice, and try as she might, she couldn't stop her body from reacting to the warm press of his leg against hers.

"I didn't explain about the fine print because I wasn't planning on asking you to sign a prenup." He settled his arm around her shoulders and pulled her close.

"But that doesn't change the fact that you don't want to have children, and I do." She tried to toughen up, but a part of her had softened and heated. Then there were the damn tears that seeped out of her eyes uninvited. "I love you—I do—but I can't marry you. It seems we're destined to hurt each other."

Amber pulled away and got to her feet. "Please say good-bye to your mum and to Bella. I really like your family, although I can't say I'm a fan of your stepmother." She rubbed her hands on her shorts, her palms sweaty. "Or your dad after speaking to Bella, but I know one thing without a doubt. You're not the man your father is. You're so much more. And unlike him, you'd make a fine father." The seepage became a torrent, and she swiped at her cheeks in frustration. Damn it.

"Are you finished?" He got to his feet and took her into his arms.

"Not yet. You have so much love to give. Any girl would be blessed to marry you. You care for your sister, your mum—you cared about the girls on the show, every single one of them—and once upon a time you cared about *me*."

"I never stopped caring about you." He kissed her forehead, and the tears ran afresh. How could he not be aware of the incredible man he was?

"You're not your father, Nate. You put your family first. You can't listen to your stepmother. If you marry, she has a lot to lose."

"So, what do you suggest I do?"

"You need a wife, and you have two beautiful women who want to marry you—but I'm not one of them. I want children. I want a family. I want to create a home. And I want to fill it with love... the way your mum fills this house with love."

"So, you're planning to walk away?"

"I think that would be best. I'll get Cassie to direct the finale because... I can't... I can't do this anymore." She wanted to curl up into a spikey ball and keep Neanderthals like Nathan a safe distance away.

He cupped her face with his hands and lifted her watery gaze to his, lowering his mouth to hers—tenderly, softly—and when his lips met hers, she was already in too much of a dither to resist. And when he pulled back, she followed him, wanting, yearning, needing.

"I fully plan to marry you, Amber Reed, if you'll have me. And I fully plan to give you those children—as many as you'd like. And I want us to stay married until the end of time—no prenup required."

His kiss left no room for argument and Amber's resistance

drained away, her heart swelling inside her chest. "Oh, I like it," she whispered. "I like it a lot."

Chapter Thirteen

N ate and Niko stood at the top of a hill in the Sydney Botanic Gardens, silhouetted against a rosy sky with the city skyline behind them, and beautiful sprawling trees in front. When the camera panned to the right, the pitch dropped away to the sea, and the Opera House came into view. The sunset was perfect, like it had been sent from heaven.

Amber held her breath as Mia arrived in a white limousine in a stunning gown, her hair gorgeously coiffed, with hope in her eyes. She looked confident and breezy as Cory moved to greet her, his voice husky as he urged her to join Nate. Amber's heartbeat ratcheted up in her chest, from fast to furious. The footage was stunning. The cameras followed Mia's steps towards Nate who looked out to sea, his hand on Niko's collar. For once, Niko stayed still as if he could sense Nate's tension.

Amber's loose dress billowed in the slight breeze, the warmth of it skating over her bare legs and sending a delicious caress across her skin. Unlike the girls, her hair was loose and pulled back with a simple band of white flowers.

She watched as Nate took Mia's hand in his and went through the carefully scripted speech. Only Nate could deliver this disappointing news in such a way that Mia would feel honoured and blessed. Perhaps he'd given her an inkling of what was to come because her reaction was raw, but there was no sign of the heart-breaking hysterics Amber had feared. Love could be cruel, but Nate was respectful and endearing, and by the time Mia turned away from him towards the waiting vehicle, Amber couldn't see through her tears. How could she do this to them? How could she let Nate go through with what he planned to do?

"Are you okay, Am?" Cassie was there and Amber nodded. Mia settled into the limo, and the cameras zoomed closer, her words poignant and sad, driving a stake of guilt into Amber's heart. Cassie squeezed her hand. "You've got this. And don't worry, the girls were paid very well to film this last episode. Trust me."

The limo turned slowly in the roadway, and Amber kept her eyes on the horizon. On Nate and Niko. When Catherine arrived, her tears welled again, and Cassie took her hand and squeezed. "All's fair in love and war," she whispered. "These women knew what they were risking. They had as much chance of winning his heart as you did. It was a fair fight."

"It wasn't a fair fight. They didn't even know I was the competition. They thought I was their friend."

"You are. You were. You supported them with an open heart. You weren't expecting this any more than they were. That's love isn't it? It strikes when you least expect it."

"Wait until they see the show. They'll understand there was no malice in this. You've done a brilliant job with the edits. The audience will want this unexpected ending. They'll be holding their breaths and desperately hoping that Nate doesn't propose to Mia or Catherine. They'll want him to do the unexpected, to be brave, and step outside of the script to propose to the woman he truly loves. They'll know that it's real. They'll want that for you and Nate. They'll want you to be together."

"I hope you're right." Amber spoke through gritted teeth, her muscles taut.

Catherine made her way along the short distance to Nate and Niko. Amber could hear Nate's breath in her ear, sharp and fast. He wasn't as calm as he pretended to be. She heard the long, deep in-breath he took to armour himself. She felt for him. He really liked these women. There was a level of intimacy between them, and her heartbeat jammed... would he change his mind at the last moment? He had every right to choose the woman who was right for him, come hell or high water. He owed her nothing. Not anymore. She wanted him to be happy. If happy was with Catherine, then so be it.

Amber listened as Nate took Catherine's hands in his and gazed into her eyes. His words shook. This wasn't a thoughtless and uncaring man. This man felt deeply. He knew his words would hurt and disappoint, and he spoke gently and kindly, with compassion.

Catherine's head lowered, and Amber saw resignation in the curve of her shoulders. How could he do this? It was hard to watch. Tears welled in Amber's eyes as she studied her handsome beau, so strong and brave, so daring as he faced the world and took the path less easy to follow. Her pulse skipped and danced and hammered in her ears. Her breath snatched at the sweetly scented spring air, so near summer now. They needed to move or lose the orange hue that permeated the light cloud in the sky. She felt the camera's eye on her, and it was something she would never get used to.

This time Nate and Niko walked Catherine back to the

limousine. His gaze was warm as he wrapped his arm around her and settled her into the back seat. He stepped away and with Niko returned to his position at the top of the rise. Not once did he look back. His eyes were on the horizon and the future.

Catherine wiped the tears from her eyes, and her words were pain-filled and disappointed, but she was happy for Mia. How devastated would she feel when she realised Nate hadn't chosen Mia either?

Amber waited until the limousine turned and drove away.

The makeup artist touched up her face and admonished her for her tears, but it didn't seem to matter how much she tried, she couldn't stop crying. It wasn't fair to take what she wanted at someone else's expense. Except that Nate's love didn't belong to the other girls. It belonged to her. This was Nate's choice. He'd made that clear when he refused to propose to Mia or Catherine. If she wanted a proposal in the finale of her show, she had to front up herself. The thought was terrifying. She was more at home behind the cameras than in front of them.

Amber stepped out onto the warmth of the grass, the scent of the earth mixing with the scent of the flowers in her hair. The grass was soft beneath her bare feet, and time slowed as she walked towards the man she loved. Her dress was a simple sheath of silk and the breeze pulled her hair away from her face. This time, Nate turned, and Niko barked. They walked towards her and there was such love on Nate's face that she couldn't shift her gaze from the cobalt blue of his, not even when the tears welled up and spilled over.

He'd removed his tie and opened the top button of his white shirt to expose his tanned and lightly haired chest. The fabric lovingly clung to his muscle and she yearned to touch. He'd abandoned the glossy black shoes he'd worn for the girls, and now his feet were bare. She smiled because she couldn't help it, even as she cried. The heat of the lights was intense, but she scarcely noticed as the distance closed between them.

Nate handed her his final key—the key to his heart—and she held it with shaky hands. It seemed like time stopped in its interminable track as he waited, his gaze loving and true before drawing her close. She breathed him in, her eyelids closing, the familiar, musky scent of him stirring her deep inside. Her mouth brushed his, and she felt his smile. He lifted her chin, and she opened her eyes to gaze deep into the clear blue promise of his. She smiled when his lips brushed hers again.

"Amber Reed. I've loved you since I was eighteen, and I will love you until I take my last breath. Will you marry me and make me the happiest man alive?"

"I will," she whispered, her vision watery, her laugh loud as Niko jumped up against her dress.

"Get down," Nate growled. "That dog has no manners. We've got a big job ahead of us."

"We do." She laughed and forgot they were being photographed, forgot the audience, forgot everything except for the man in front of her. "I can't wait to marry you."

"I'm glad to hear it." He grinned. "Because I can't wait to marry you either." He lowered his mouth to hers.

"Cut, that's brilliant," Cassie called, but Amber didn't hear her and neither did Nate.

* * *

Thank you so much for reading *Bachelor on Board!* I hope you enjoyed Amber and Nate's story. Bachelor on Board is from my 'Beauty and the Bachelor' box set—a collection of standalone stories based on the Beauty and the Beast trope!!

Amber believes success is the best revenge. In truth, *no revenge is the best revenge. Move on. Be happy. Find inner peace. Flourish.* I love affirmations and this one is from @peacefulmindpeacef ullife. Forgiveness is the highest form of self-love... Holding on to negative emotions harms us more than the person who wronged us.

If you enjoyed *Bachelor on Board,* I'd really appreciate a review on your Amazon website of choice and/or on Goodreads: https://www.goodreads.com/book/show/41014887-desert-prince-scandalous-affair. Authors rely on readers' reviews to stand out (hopefully in a good way)!

And if you'd like to join my newsletter and receive a free welcome gift (Bachelor on Trial), I'd love to see you at: https://d l.bookfunnel.com/lzmhskru7g

I'd love to hear from you! You can find me at www.lexi-greene.com.au.

Or on Facebook at www.facebook.com/lexi.greene.75 or www.facebook.com/lovelexigreene.

Warmest regards,

Lexi xx

About the Author

About the Author

Lexi is an Australian author who loves to write powerful, passionate and provocative stories. She writes romance in the early morning and works as a paediatric neuropsychologist by day. A happily married mum of two teens, a parrot and a puppy, she loves to escape into a good story. She is a firm believer that a bath, a green tea and chocolate take a good book and make it perfect.

Lexi is a member of Romance Writers of Australia and Romance Writers of America; and is a huge fan of Margie Lawson's Writer's Academy.

Lexi loves a good happily ever after...

Also by Lexi Greene

Bachelor on Trial
When Tony Radcliff joins Forbes lawyers, career-driven Scarlet O'Connor finds she has competition for the coveted senior associate position.

And Tony has a couple of aces up his sleeve. Like his surf-sculpted body, which plays havoc with Scarlet's 'all work and no play' plans for partnership. And his brother, who holds the key to a secret from her past.

When Scarlet and Tony start steaming up the office windows, there's no doubt they're playing with fire. But there can only be one winner, so who gets burned?

https://books2read.com/Bachelor-On-Trial

Bachelor on Guard

Abby Kercher has spent the past five years proving she doesn't need Nico D'Antoni, but now her life is in danger and Nico is the only man who can keep her safe.

Abby is all grown up and Nico finds she's changed in dangerous ways, but some things haven't changed, like their unwanted attraction, the darkness of his past, and his promise to protect her, which must override everything.

Can they put their past behind them, or will a long-kept secret destroy them both?

https://books2read.com/Bachelor-On-Guard

Shatterproof

Emily Stone, an internationally successful model on the brink of supermodel stardom, appears to have it all. All, except love, because Emily wants the kind of man who isn't fooled by the pretty. She wants the kind of love that's big enough and true enough to include her disabled sister and dysfunctional mother.

Nick was an A-list actor in tinsel town with a super-sized ego until a tragic car accident stole his wife, his unborn child, and his gilded career, leaving him physically and emotionally scarred.

When wintry French Island brings these two wayward souls home, shared childhood memories aren't enough to bridge the deep divide forged by their adult lives and choices.

That is until Carmie, Emily's delightful Down Syndrome sister, weaves her special kind of magic. Can Carmie's boundless love and infectious joy help them to heal their broken hearts or will the glamour of Emily's work-world whisk her away?

https://books2read.com/Heart-of-Glass-Shatterpoof

Desert Prince, Scandalous Affair

There is nothing Zahidah's Prince Rashid bin Ra'ed Al Shahid won't do to safeguard his family's honour and his kingdom's future.

And there is nothing Jemma Mason won't do to protect her daughter, Sami, the result of a crazy one-night connection with a dark, handsome cliché in a Sydney bar.

When Sami needs a bone-marrow transplant, Princess Aminah, Rashid's sister, steps in to save Sami's life and promises to keep Jemma's secret. There is nothing Jemma won't do for Aminah including rescuing her from an arranged marriage she dreads.

When Aminah is abducted, Prince Rashid wants answers and his questions lead him to Jemma and her web of lies.

Jemma can't resist Rashid's scandalous proposal, but can he forgive her when he discovers the truth?

https://books2read.com/Desert-Prince-Scandalous-Affair

Once Upon a Christmas Wish

Jenn Adams is determined to tick off her bucket list and face her past nemeses—learning to ski and a man named Brad.

Brad Oregon is the only man she's ever loved. His chocolate eyes. His to-die-for smile. His toned body. His very toned body.

But Brad's reputation with women is almost as renowned as his ski-racing success. Now a ski instructor in beautiful Whistler, he's as difficult to resist as the scenery! What the hell. Life is short. A two-week holiday romance should suit them both perfectly. Right?

https://books2read.com/Once-Upon-A-Christmas-Wish